My Name Is
Thank-You

My Name Is Thank-You

A Novel

Kaizen Love

My Name Is Thank-You
A novel by Kaizen Love

Book design by Maureen Cutajar
www.gopublished.com

Thanks Dad.

"No one's life should be rooted in fear. We are born for wonder, for joy, for hope, for love, to marvel at the mystery of existence, to be ravished by the beauty of the world, to seek truth and meaning, to acquire wisdom, and by our treatment of others to brighten the corner where we are."

—*Life Expectancy* by Dean Koontz.

Contents

Prologue

I ain't never met my mama, except that one time when she was pushing me out of her belly, but I don't really remember that day much. I can recall hearing a lot of crying, but none of it was coming from me. I think when I was born, I came into the world with a smile on my face, because that's what Miss Felix, my social-worker mama, tell me all the time. She tell me that before I was born God took a paintbrush to my face and decorated it special, just for me. And God knew that I was gonna be born on a sad day, so He or She put a big pretty smile on me so nobody would ever know what sadness was when I was around. That's what my social-worker mama say to me all the time.

She say my mama named me Thank-You because she wanted me to know how grateful she was that she got to meet me before she went to Heaven. But me, I think it's because she always wanted me to mind my manners like mamas do, and never forget to say thank you. If my mama was alive, she would be proud because I always saying thank you, and not just because it's my name.

JOSEPHINE

Sometimes the sun is the only thing that makes me feel alive. I try to trace my shadow along the ground, but it doesn't stop moving. I just wish it would stop for a second so that I could talk to it, ask it why it hides its face from me; why it's always so dark and elusive. I feel like my shadow is my best friend, even if it won't speak to me.

The worst feeling in the world is loneliness. Some people disagree with that, but really that's the truth. There is nothing else like it in the world. I have my mother and my father, but they barely speak to each other let alone me. Father doesn't love me, and Mother loves the bottle more than anything else. I just don't want to end up with some tragic story like some of the women I read about in my books. But I feel like it's inevitable. Mother says I was born a curse, my name a reminder of what I will never be, the boy that they married for, dreamt of, and will never meet.

PART ONE

Summer

1.

Thank-You

All babies is born for a purpose, whether they ever realize it or not I reckon is they own business. By the time we fall out from between our mamas' thighs things already been set into motion that propel us forward toward our destiny. From that first moment when our little bodies hit the coldness of life and we scream to be put back into that warm cozy cocoon, that's when our journey start. Some of us is lucky enough to take that journey with people that care for us, love us, and protect us. While the rest of us, well I reckon the rest of us busy trying to figure it out on our own.

No matter how long each human bean exist on this earth, we all want to be a part of something. We all want a place that's special just for us, where we belong. Orphaned kids like me usually don't find it till they get adopted. Some find it through religion, holding on to the idea of God being they daddy, and others find it out on the street, where their friends become the only family they got. For me, I'm still waiting to find it at all.

It ain't been easy not knowing what it's like to have a family. The kind where everybody resemble each other, where the mama and daddy tuck the baby girl into bed to read her a bedtime story till she fall asleep. The kind where the little girl got brothers and sisters that she could play with, tell secrets with, and sometimes even fight with. I'm thirteen years old now, and I know fighting wrong, but I still wish I had somebody I could fight with. Just so when fighting time done we could hug and be best friends like we ain't never had the fight in the first place. That's the problem with lots of people; they don't appreciate the little things. Things like having family to fight with. All they busy concerning themselves with is the fight itself and un-forgiveness. I forgave my mama for leaving me, and she ain't even here to receive it.

I pray for that a lot, for the kind of love I could only get from a real-life family; for the feeling that I belong to something special. I'm not saying that I ain't never received no kind of love, because it come in many forms. I got my social-worker mama, Miss Felix, and she been my social worker for as long as I can remember ever having a memory. A social-worker mama is a real special type. That's the kind that even though she ain't play no part in bringing me into this world, she check in on me to make sure I getting fed good, keeping clean, and ain't nobody hitting on me. And she work real hard to try to find a nice family to adopt me. I only see her a couple times a week, sometimes less than that if she real busy helping other kids like me.

I think she show me extra love because she been with me for so long. A lot of the other kids get switched around to all different kinds of social-worker mamas. I hear lots of them complaining 'bout how they never get nobody nice, one that even remember they names, and could care less 'bout the kind of fake families they put them to stay with. But not me, I got me the most amazing social-worker mama in the world. Sometimes I wonder if my real-life mama sent her to me.

Miss Felix got pretty chocolate skin, her kinky hair always tied back in a little, tight bun that be making her dark brown eyes look real open, like she be using her bun to keep herself awake. She a little bit short and real meaty, with ankles that love her legs so much, you can't even tell 'em apart. And my favorite thing of all, she got the kindest eyes I ever seen. She got the kind of eyes that look at you like they thinking everything 'bout you is special.

She always real sweet with me, saying things like, "Baby girl, God does listen extra hard to you cuz of yo name and cuz of how much you does love to smile." I don't even know why it is I smile so much. Maybe it's because I like how my cheeks feel when they stretch out real big and wide. I can almost make both corners of my mouth touch my ears. Or maybe I do it for my teeth? They feel so nice when the wind hits them. They get bored in my mouth since they stuck in there all the time. The least I could do is let them feel the wind as often as I can, because they help me eat food every day, and it's nice to do things to show appreciation.

It's Sunday morning, and usually on Sunday mornings we get to sleep in a little late before the morning bell ring letting us know it's time to open up our eyes and get fixed up to eat breakfast in the dining hall. We have prayer time too. That's when somebody teach us how to pray, and we learn from the scriptures and sing songs real loud. Some people even run about the place stomping they feet and talking real funny. It's almost like going to church, except ain't nobody get fancied up.

I like that part of Sundays the best, because I like listening to them stories 'bout all them people in the Bible. Sometimes they

7

make me wish I was born back in them times so that I could have been best friends with Jesus. I don't think he would have played fighting with me though, because the Bible say that God was his real-life daddy. Can you imagine getting a whooping from God? If God was my real-life daddy, I wouldn't want no whooping from him. One of my fake mamas tell me once she was gonna "spank the bejesus outta me." Naturally being a curious kind of child, I responded, "If you gonna be spanking Jesus outta me, what in Heaven's name God gonna be spanking outta Jesus?" I got a real good whooping that day, and she ain't never answered my question.

Today is a special kind of Sunday; Miss Felix is picking me up this morning. She don't ever come round here on a weekend, especially to pick me up from my home. It's not really my home, like the ones the real-life families live in, the one we was talking about earlier with the brothers and sisters and mamas and daddies, but it's a place for other little girls like me, ones that ain't got no family. I call it "home" because it's where I keep all my things. My baby dolls is here, my clothes is here, and the picture I drew of my real-life mama is here. Even though it ain't the kind of home that other people got, it do a good job of keeping me safe, warm, and out of trouble.

I'm not real sure why Miss Felix picking me up. I got woke up by the weekend caretaker almost as early as the sun get up, telling me I need to be up and dressed by eight o'clock and ready for my social worker who was coming to get me. I was too excited to bother asking any questions. That's even before the wake-up bell supposed to ring. None of that matter much. I'm so happy to be going out, I don't care how much sleep I could still be sleeping. I know that Miss Felix don't got no babies of her own, but I know she married because she got a ring on her married-people finger, so I can't imagine why she not spending the day with her husband. If it was me, and I was married, and had a home for all my baby dolls I don't think I would ever go nowhere on a Sunday.

I spend my morning getting ready, tossing on the only pair of pants that fit me right and a used t-shirt with no stains that I recently acquired from a new box of donations. That's a rare find round here. My mind thinking of all the different reasons she could have for spending her Sunday with me. The only one that make the most sense is that she found another place for me to stay for a while. Another place where a strange lady is gonna try to dress me up like one of my baby dolls so she could take me round her church friends and round her family. Where her strange husband gonna try bouncing me up and down on his knee till I start feeling sick and throw up breakfast, lunch, or dinner all over his freshly shined shoes.

Sometimes I think that when people sign up to take kids like me with no mamas and daddies they think they always getting cute little babies. But when they meet me, I could always see the disappointment in they eyes. It's like even though they know I's thirteen years old, and I'm sure Miss Felix done describe me to them, I think they still expecting to meet a three-year-old baby girl. One with rosy cheeks, strawberry-filled baskets in her hands, eyes sparkling like diamonds, and a name like Amber or Georgina, something pretty like that. Instead they get me, Thank-You. Miss Felix say I'm something special to look at, and I'm the reason that she know God like to get creative with us human beans and show how "beautiful" don't have to look no type of way, it just is. I'm a bit small for my age, with the skinniest little legs, Miss Felix call them my "walking sticks." I got short hair, a mixture of brown tangled together with blonde. It's curly and thick and as hard as running your fingers through a sheep's wool. My eyes blue like staring directly into the heart of the ocean with skin the color of toffee covered in the tiniest chocolate-chip-sprinkle freckles.

When I walk into the room to meet my new fake families, all they tend to do is stare. And soon as Miss Felix leave they try making me look like how they thinking I should look. Like they own the definition of the word "beautiful." Putting all kinds of stuff in my hair to try get it flat and straight, makeup covering up all my chocolate chips. At least they think my eyes is pretty. Miss Felix told me after the last family demanded that I get picked up because "I just didn't fit in," that she was only gonna take me to a family that would understand how special I was. They was gonna love me and not get annoyed by me all the time, or try to burn me, hit me, cuss at me, pour liquor down my throat, or even put tape on my mouth so I don't ask no questions I ain't supposed to.

I'm making sure all my stuff is put away neat so when she get here we could just go. I know if I ain't ready she gonna come inside and she gonna ask me if I ate breakfast, so I best be ready to just jump in her car, so I don't gotta lie. Because I ain't no good at lying at all. I don't like how the wrong words feel when they coming out of my mouth. It's like my teeth don't even wanna help me push them lies out, so I tell the truth. That way we all happy. But, it's tempting to lie to Miss Felix because she always asking so many questions; she especially like to ask if I'm eating all my meals.

It's not that I don't like food, because I do, I love food, and I love what it do for my body every day. I love that food give me enough energy to keep my eyes open to see the pretty flowers that bloom in springtime. I love that food smell so good it make my mouth get real watery and juicy. I love how food taste except for when I have to eat celery and peas. I know God made them too, but I don't think they was made for me. And, I love how food feel on my tongue, especially real slimy food—that's my favorite, like okra. It seem like all the other little boys and girls that live in my home is always complaining about the food: they complain about how the food be smelling, they complain about how the food be looking, and they complain about how the food be tasting. That don't make no kind of sense to me, because it ain't like they got other mamas and daddies cooking better food for them no place else. They don't even say anything to the nice people that be cooking for them all day. Every time I get food I always tell everybody "thank you," even on them days when we get celery and peas, and the nice old ladies smile and they say back, "Thank you, Thank-You." Then I smile at them, take my food, and politely walk away, shoving as much of it as I can into my pockets.

See, even though I love me a good meal, I don't always eat them. I don't waste or nothing, I just got me a small, little, furry secret. I got me a friend, and his name is Grandma. I know that's a funny name for a squirrel, especially a boy squirrel at that, but I thought it would be nice to say, "I gotta go see Grandma," all the time. Like when somebody say, "Where you going, Thank-You?" I say back to them, "To feed Grandma." And saying that make me feel good, and that make my teeth feel happy because I smile so big when I say it, they get to feel the wind again. Miss Felix don't like that I be giving my food away to Grandma. She say it's wasteful because squirrels eat wild-animal food like acorns and nuts and things like that. But Miss Felix don't know that Grandma love my food. He even eating out of my hand now, and he ain't never even tried to bite me. All Grandma do is love me. And that's enough for me to bring him as many of my meals as I can.

2.

Josephine

Everybody has his or her own definition of what it means to be lonely. Some will never know what it feels like to be stained by its darkness, while others are fated to live a life so rich with it that it creates a thickness around the very core of who they are. It's hard to imagine your true potential when you are weighed down by thirteen years of loneliness. For me, that has been my entire lifetime.

I've had many people tell me that I should feel blessed coming from the family that I do. My father is one of the most influential black men in this part of the south, and you better believe he acts like it too. We come from what they call "old money." That means that my father inherited his wealth from his father, who inherited it from his father and so forth. I'm not sure where the money originated from, or which one of my ancestors made it possible for me to wear fancy dresses every day, go to the best schools, or eat off of the best china to be found in any part of the world. But here I am, Josephine Dieu. I don't even know how I got a last name meaning "God," but I do. Sometimes I wonder if one of my ancestors just made it up so they could feel powerful, like all that money they got wasn't enough.

I can't even imagine what it would be like to be poor. I don't say this because I look down on poor people. I just see them all of the time, these strange folks. I see them as I'm riding in the car with my father and mother. Mother tells me not to stare, but I can't help it. I think that there is something about being poor that is so beautiful. The kids around my age are always so happy. I don't even know what they could possibly be smiling about, but there they go showing off each and every tooth, living in the worst neighborhoods with the dirtiest, ugliest clothes I have ever seen. Their parents all wear big smiles too, except most of them have already lost their teeth by the time they are twenty-five. I don't know if I'll ever understand it. I guess I can't imagine what it would be like to be poor, because I can't imagine what it would be like to be happy like them.

Mother and Father say that people are poor because they are lazy, and they choose to not do any better for themselves. I personally don't think that's true, because poor people could say that my rich father is lazy since he didn't earn a penny of his money himself. I think a whole lot about things like that, and about life in general. I don't do much talking because at my age no one really thinks I have much to say. But I do. When you are quiet, you are able to see all the things about the world that other people are busy hollering about.

Mother and Father are always hollering. They holler at me, at each other, or at the people they have working for them. As a matter of fact, I think the only time I hear their voices is when they are hollering. Besides that, they don't talk to me very much at all. I wonder all of the time what it would be like to be a part of a family that is loving, one that likes to go to the park and take long walks together, one that likes to talk about what went on during their day, or one that likes to give hugs and kisses to their baby girl. But that's just not how it is with us.

When Mother is drinking she likes to explain how I came to be a part of their family, born into their world. I take advantage of these moments, because when she's good and drunk she talks more than she hollers, and I listen every time with a glimmer of hope in my eyes that she may slip and say something nice. Unfortunately, it seems as if she makes a deliberate effort to never sugarcoat anything, and she never has. "Josephine, life is full of jagged edges," she says with a liquor-soaked tongue, "and if I tell you anything otherwise you are going to end up stepping on every single one, thinking that they are as soft as clouds. So if I tell you something, girl, it's for your own damn good."

By the time she is on her third or fourth drink, she repeats the same story unfailingly—the story of my "curse." Mother says that I was born cursed because my father wanted to have a baby so badly he convinced her to run away with him to get married in secret without getting her parents' approval. It began, like most marriages, as a fairytale. She was so in love with him, they got married in the winter and by spring she was pregnant with me. I was supposed to make my father the happiest man on the face of this big old earth. Except, I was not the baby that he wanted. Coming from a long line of first-born sons, he naturally assumed that his firstborn would be a boy. Suddenly, the fairytale was over for them. Father was so angry that he was given a girl when all he wanted was a Joseph Junior. Another man that he could pass the family business down to, as well as the pride of the family name. He never forgave mother for bringing me into this world.

Soon after I was born both of mother's parents died, and at the funeral for one of them Mother overheard one of the deacons in the church saying that they died of shame. At this point my parents had already labeled me a curse, and as if that wasn't bad enough, when Mother tried to get pregnant again she discovered that during my birth something happened to her baby-making parts, and she was unable to have any more babies.

Can you believe that while all of this was going on my little baby self went unnamed? That's right. Mother said that they didn't have any girl names prepared because they were certain to have a boy. They were so busy with the funeral arrangements for her parents and the devastation of learning the news of her broken baby parts, that they plum forgot to name me. They had the help call me "the baby" and nothing else until she eventually thought that by naming me Josephine after Father, he would grow to love me. But Father never did. As a matter of fact, he barely even acknowledges me when I walk into a room. Sometimes he'll look up from his newspaper, but mainly it's just to check to see if it's someone worth talking to.

Can you imagine being named after somebody that doesn't even like you? Worst yet, I look just like my father. We are both shorter than average and thin, eyes light and rich like honey flowing fresh from a beehive, cheek bones gifted directly from an Egyptian queen sitting high on her throne, and hair soft and kinky, that grows up instead of down. The only resemblances that I have to my mother is the cinnamon color that tints our skin and the freckles that dance around our eyes, gracefully along the curves of our cheeks.

I've done lots of things over the years to try to get my parents to love me, but I'm beginning to realize that it's a hopeless battle. I can't cry myself to sleep forever, and besides, the only thing I have ever really known of love was by seeing people on the cinema screen or by going to the park on a Saturday morning and watching how other families interact with each other: the parents playing with their babies, everybody laughing, getting dirty, and having a good time. Sometimes I fall asleep wishing that I had a brother. Someone that I could play with or talk to, but mainly someone who would take away this curse and make me loveable. I never pray for a sister, that would be selfish, poor thing would be just as cursed as me.

I pray often for God to fix mother's broken baby parts so that she can have a boy for Father. I've even gone to my Aunt Clara's house to ask for her help. Aunt Clara isn't really my aunt, she's just a lady that lives in our neighborhood, but where we come from anybody that is older than you is either aunt, uncle, sir, ma'am, miss, or mister. Sometimes Aunt Clara fixes potions for women when their husbands stop coming home at night. I know that because one day I went with mother to get a potion for Father and I listened as Aunt Clara gave her all the instructions on how to use the potion. First, she told Mother she had to take a sip of a separate potion herself. "Now, you only take a sip, you hear? Outta this smaller vial. That's to make you brave. Then you gonna make a pitcher of lemonade so sweet he gonna wanna be greedy and drink it all up himself. That's a trait all selfish men got, but make sure you let everyone know that this a special lemonade only for your husband. Because you ain't want nobody getting they hands on this batch here. Then you gonna mix in the whole bigger vile, getting every last drop into that sweet juice." She told

Mother that the potion would make Father stay home at night, and would give her the confidence she needed to ask him all the questions she had. Questions that were taking up all the space in her mind.

I'm pretty sure the potion worked on Father. I watched Mother carefully as she made that sweet-smelling lemonade. That juice looked so tempting if I didn't know that it was full of potion I would have snuck some for myself. I heard the screaming and yelling for a couple of nights as Mother asked Father all she wanted, and to my surprise he didn't leave the house for almost two weeks. But as soon as that lemonade and potion was just a memory, he stopped coming home again.

After seeing how powerful Miss Clara's potions were I took a walk to her house so I could ask her if she could make a potion for me. I didn't quite know what to ask her, or what to say when I got there, but I knew that I had to be brave and at least try. When I got to her house I nervously approached her front door. Aunt Clara has a big, beautiful house. It's not as big as ours, but she has the most beautiful yellow moonbeam flowers lining the walkway up to her front door. Fortunately, when I approached she was already outside, sitting on her front porch rocking back and forth in her rocking chair. That chair looked as if it were forged from the bones of every woman who has sat in it before her, women whose blood and tears mingled and danced together to make Aunt Clara possible.

When I saw her sitting there I almost lost all of my gumption. I croaked out in one big burst of breath, "Aunt Clara, afternoon, ma'am. Um, I um, I need a potion for Mother because God was supposed to make me a boy, but I was a girl, and I broke her baby-making parts, so I need a potion to fix her so she can have a son so

Father will come home at night and they will love me, and we will be better." That was the fastest words have ever left my mouth. Aunt Clara just stared as I took a deep gasp of air. She didn't respond; she just stared at me and rocked. Nervously, I kept on talking. I offered her all of the money that I got from working with my uncle at his bookshop over the past few summers. Money that I'd been saving so that one day I could have my own big pretty house, and fill it with more love than my parents have stuff.

After marinating on my words for a few more moments Aunt Clara softly and sympathetically said, "I'm sorry, baby girl, in matters like that I ain't no one to mess with the hand of God, I'm sorry that you think you ain't loved by yo mama and yo daddy, but God don't be making no mistakes. It's best not to blame God for grown folks' selfish ways, everything always coming back full circle in this life. One minute you thinking life one way, the next it done completely changed. Just wait on God, baby." I left Aunt Clara's house sad and disappointed that day, walking home extra slowly and wondering why the hand of God would do something like make my mother unable to give my father a son, or why God would make me a girl knowing that I would be born to parents that wouldn't love me.

I walked home with my head hanging down so low to the ground, I could not only smell the fresh cut grass, but I could taste the rich brown soil that nourished it. The same soil that stares in horror, watching its babies get mowed and plowed and stepped on by folks that don't pay attention. I was low, feeling like that grass, not because Aunt Clara didn't make me the potion, but because she told me that God doesn't make mistakes. And it was breaking my heart to think that God, the same God that exists in my name, is either real mean, or really good at telling lies, because, I am here, and I am clearly a mistake.

3.

Thank-You

Miss Felix pulled up in front of the home, luckily I was smart enough to get my stuff all put away so that I could run out to the car and jump right in. "Good morning, ma'am," I say politely and a bit out of breath from my sprint down the sidewalk. "Well good morning, Thank-You, baby. You run over here awfully quick for such a tiny little thing with tiny little legs. How they bring you over here so fast?" I couldn't help but giggle. I knew she was just busting my chops a bit, even though I do got tiny little legs.

I think Miss Felix is a good social-worker mama, and would be an even better real-life mama because she real sensible. I think she already knew that I wasn't gonna be able to lie to her if she asked me if I'd eaten breakfast. So instead of asking, she just handed me a small pouch with a peanut butter sandwich and the cutest little apple juice box. I was so excited my "thank you" came out a bit higher pitched than usual. I didn't even realize how hungry I actually was till that delicious peanut butter hit the roof of my mouth, and before I could stop my teeth they devoured the whole entire thing in just about seven seconds. Sometimes my teeth get way more excited than I do 'bout stuff, but this time I think we was on the same page.

By the time Miss Felix pulled away from the curb, my breakfast was nothing but a delicious memory. I folded up my empty juice box, and put it into the plastic pouch that once held my sandwich. Miss Felix always like it when I am neat and tidy. She say that more people in this world need to be neat and tidy; maybe if they was, then we would all live better together. She say ain't nobody like coming home to a dirty house, so why must we keep our whole big world dirty?

I think Miss Felix real smart and wise. She always sharing her beliefs with me 'bout how people live in this world. She know from firsthand experience, because she done traveled to a couple places outside the South already. She tell me stories sometimes that make me sad, like how people killing off all the animals in the world with something called pollution. That's when people don't got no kind of sense. They minds get diseased and they spread it to the earth and the earth spread it to the animals, and everything die off. She say if people not careful we all gonna die off one day too, cuz everything come back full circle.

"Miss Felix, we been driving for a while now, could you tell me where we going, ma'am?" Miss Felix got a kind of look on her face that I ain't never quite seen before. It was a face like I get when I find an old penny on the floor. I love finding old pennies. It's my favorite gift to find. I think God be leaving them round for me, because He or She know just how much I love them. I ain't got nothing against new pennies; it's just old pennies make me feel something special in my belly. Even though it's the same picture ol the same man sitting on that penny, his eyes always looking different. The older that penny get, the deeper that man eyes see into my soul, and through his eyes each penny teach me something new 'bout myself. In this moment, Miss Felix looking just like me, when I'm standing over a rusty, old penny, eyes glistening like it's a chunk of gold.

"Thank-You, baby, we headed on out to church this morning." I could feel the excitement bursting out of her mouth, and I wonder if talking 'bout church does make Miss Felix's teeth happy. It must, because I could see all of them with that big ole smile she smiling, the missing ones in the back and all. They must love the wind as much as mine do because Miss Felix like to smile too. I understand why she smiling so big. I do love going to church. I have been to so many churches all over this part of the South, each one looking just like the next, sounding just like the next, the familiarity of 'em all comforting in its own little way.

Every time I get a new fake mama and daddy the first thing they do is take me to church. They take me so they can show me off to their congregation. So people can tell them how blessed they are for taking in a "different kind of orphan" like me. I still don't know exactly what they mean by different. Miss Felix say that people say those things because here in the South, where we come from, you is either black or you is white, but me, I don't know what I is. She say I is the exception to all that, because I ain't got to choose sides. I'm just me.

One time I was playing outside in front of the home, and a little white boy with his white daddy drove by and yelled out "half-breed." I smiled at them and waved. For the first time somebody gave me a clue to what I was; I just don't know what my halves be consisting of. When I told Miss Felix 'bout it, she just shook her head and say, "Baby girl, don't pay none of them words no mind because we all gotta come from somewhere. It don't matter what color skin you got, what color your eyes is, as long as you is alive. We all get burned by the sun and wet by the rain." When she say that she remind me of why I like going to church because hearing all that talk 'bout people dying and going to hell make me happy to be alive. I like going too because some churches ask me to stand up before they start preaching so that I could say hello to everybody, and I get to share my smile with them. I think that's my real favorite part.

As we drive, I notice out the dusty windows of Miss Felix's old beat-up car that the scenery is changing. We driving out of the areas where the houses all broken down, where car parts lay scattered across the barely there lawns, dogs running recklessly after cars with people in 'em they don't even know. The longer we drive, the prettier the scenery get. We drive past big open fields with rows of Southern Magnolia trees, recognized by many round here as a symbol for gracefulness and strength, reminding me that summer is here and overflowing with flowers so pretty they making me blush.

I ain't never seen sights so beautiful like this before. The longer we drive, the more perfect the picture get as it unfolds right before my very eyes, renewing my spirit with each passing glance of something new. I ask Miss Felix if I could roll my window all the way down, and she say yes. As soon as that fresh air overtake my senses and engulf my small little world I feel my cheeks get wet. My tears warm the thin layer of skin they caress as they roll on down, passing every freckle on my cheek on their journey toward my neck.

Miss Felix, feeling the mood in the car shift from exciting to somber, look over at me and say, "Thank-You, why on earth you crying, baby?" I don't know how to explain it to her. I don't even know if the words will make sense as they slowly make their way out of my soul, assembling on my tongue to speak about things I ain't never seen, to speak about faith. I say, "Miss Felix, I'm crying because I feel like if we stopped driving the car and walked over into that field of trees bursting with all them flowers, we may realize that we ain't never need go to church again. Because God lives in the beauty of all those things, in every flower born on every tree. Like God lives in every one of my freckles, or in the eyes of every baby you help, like me."

Miss Felix looked stunned for a moment, and I thought she was gonna say that I was blasphemous, because I been told that before by other fake mamas and daddies when I say something that don't make sense to them 'bout God. But instead, my social-worker mama let out a small sigh and allowed her kind eyes to embrace the tears that gently rose their way up from the well that dwells deep within her soul. She put my hand in hers, and we continued our drive all the way to church in silence, appreciating each other, our tears, and appreciating the God that don't live inside the church building, instead, embracing the God that we find on the way there.

4.

Josephine

For the most part, my days all roll into each other. I wake up early, get myself dressed for the day, and eat breakfast with my parents in silence—sometimes, just Mother if Father doesn't come home. I walk myself down the street to the corner where the infamous Juniper Trace meets with the rest of the world. I wait for the bus to pick me up to carry me wherever it is I need to go. I used to have a driver take me around, but Father says I need to learn independence and responsibility, so now it's always just the bus or my bicycle, even when it's raining. I'm not quite sure how taking the bus teaches me any of these things, but I guess when your parents aren't the parenting types, they hand over the responsibility of teaching you life's valuable lessons to life itself. They expect that tossing me out into the world early will teach me independence and responsibility, my nanny when I was a baby to teach me about nurture and discipline, and the church to teach me about God. Everything else I learn from watching how they operate and doing the exact opposite, which leaves nothing left for them to teach me about.

The only day of the week I truly enjoy with my parents is Sunday. As a matter of fact, I wake up every Sunday morning with more happiness than I can muster through the entire week. Sunday mornings mean the sound of music vibrating through the air as it winds its way down the aisles of the churches, out of their front doors, bursting onto the street where it invites people to come and fellowship with each other, to sing, to dance, to clap, and be joyful. Everyone is on his or her best behavior today, especially Mother and Father.

Where we come from, Sunday mornings are about putting on your most expensive shoes, your fanciest hat covered in flowers and peacock feathers, and all kinds of other animal parts. To be honest some just look downright crazy. But it's all part of the show. Mother and Father love to get dressed up, and sometimes they even match. Around here, we call it wearing your Sunday best, and let me tell you, that is the truth. I have my "Sunday best" outfits too. I have socks with more frills than a tablecloth, dresses with so many beads I can barely run around with the other children, it's so heavy. And so many hats we have a separate room in the house just to keep all of them in. But that's not why I get so excited on Sunday morning.

Today, I get to experience, even if only for a few hours what it feels like to have a happy family. Driving up to the church the atmosphere in the car is always the same, Father listening to his favorite radio station with old, grumpy men talking about politics and the stock market. Mother staring at herself in the reflection of the visor mirror trying to see if Jesus still in there after drinking like a louse the night before. And me, I'm waiting to catch a glimpse of the beautiful flowers that line the pathway that lead almost directly into the church.

Once we park the car and step out into the church parking lot, Mother and Father change. All of a sudden, all three of us are holding hands walking into the church building. My parents get to feel important as they hear people say, "That Dieu family is always looking so pretty," or "That beautiful family sure is blessed," and I get to feel both of their hands in mine. Mother's hands are soft like a well-made silk scarf, although they are never warm or particularly inviting; they are hers and they are touching mine. My father's hands are firm, but unlike Mother's sometimes his are warm and almost gentle. He never squeezes my hand or pulls me. His hand just holds mine, and in these moments, we exist as a family.

When I was much younger, I just took everything as it was. I didn't have the sense to ask questions or wonder why certain things were the way they were. I just accepted, because it's all I knew. But now that I'm growing up, I have questions of all sorts, ones that I really want the answers to. Questions like, why do my parents only act like this on a Sunday? I wonder if it's because it's God's house, and they don't want to be disrespectful. Or, if it's just that they don't want God to see what they are really like, so that they make it into Heaven. Because from what I understand their money is no good there, and they just can't buy their way in. But from what I've been learning in Sunday school I have an understanding that God sees all things at all times. Like before all these people even got dressed in their Sunday best this morning, God saw them when they was still ugly. And that's what Mother and Father don't understand, that God sees them when they are being ugly in the house all throughout the week, in the car all the way here, up until that moment when their feet touch the pavement and they both grab my hand.

That's one of the things I don't understand about people. We are always thinking that others can't see just how fake we are. I mean really, if we are bold enough to think that we are walking around fooling God, then what are people? It's one of the reasons why I don't make the extra effort to smile if I don't feel like it, or cry when the tears aren't real. People are always asking, "Josephine, why do you look so sad?" And I just shrug my shoulders, because if they really wanted to know they would stop asking and start paying attention. They would watch the way my father watches the other women in the church, the way he hugs them and not my mother. They would watch the way they sit just a little bit extra away from me, because as fake as they can be, it's just not natural for them to sit too close to me. They would notice the tears falling from my eyes as we drive away from the church house every Sunday. But people don't bother paying attention. Instead, they ask questions that they don't even really want the answers to.

5.

Thank-You

I fell asleep on the drive to church, my face still a bit sticky with the tears that have now dried. It took us probably a bit over an hour to reach our destination. As we got closer Miss Felix woke me up. "Thank-You, time to get up now, baby girl. We almost reaching the church." I jumped up with enthusiasm, realizing that I didn't get to ask Miss Felix why we were coming here in the first place. I didn't want to sound ungrateful or nothing, but it's unusual for my social-worker mama to bring me to church on a Sunday morning. And not just any church. As we pull up to the massive white building, I realize that I ain't never seen another church like this.

It was looking like something out of a dream. It had a super high up pointy roof looking like they trying to make the church reach up to Heaven, big windows so people walking by could see all the holiness that going on inside, and the pathway leading up to the doors was surrounded by the most beautiful flowers I have ever seen. I figured at this point, asking why we was here wasn't an important question to ask after all, because we is meant to be where we is meant to be in every moment. It don't matter the reason why we are here, what matter is, that we are here.

As we pull into the parking lot, I notice that most of the cars are much fancier than Miss Felix's own. As a matter of fact, all of the houses around the church were looking like museums, and courthouses, and such. It was such a spectacular sight to witness and for the first time ever in the history of my life, I think I was nervous. I don't even quite know why I was so nervous, I just know that I was gettin' butterflies all up through my belly, and they were bubbling in such a way that my freckles was rising up from under my skin, and forming goose pimples. I had so many all up and down my arms I thought I was fixing to grow feathers and fly away.

I ain't never had no goose pimples like that in my life. I thought you could only get them when you was fixing to throw up or when you was really cold. Like that time I was staying with a fake family and they took my only sweater to give it to their real-life daughter, saying she needed it more than me because she was littler, and it was freezing outside. I had so many goose pimples for those couple of weeks, by the time Miss Felix came to check up on me I had me a bad case of pneumonia. And even today, I got more goose pimples than I did then.

Miss Felix looked over at me, and she must have felt my nerves racing through my body, because she gently rubbed my arm till all my pimples went down. She didn't even have to say nothing, because we both knew that we were here for a reason. One that could have only been aligned by the stars, by fate, the universe, or God, or whatever your name be for the divine hand that guides us all down the path to our ultimate destiny.

As we parked the car, I pulled down the small, dusty and cracked visor mirror that hung crooked over my head. I ain't never had much concern 'bout my appearance before, but watching all them people walk into that church with they fancy outfits, make me feel some type of way 'bout my outfit. I didn't know we was coming to a church, let alone one this fancy. Although, it's not like if I knew I would have done anything different. I only got but one dress, one pair of blue jeans, and two t-shirts. I don't got my sweater no more, so that's all I own. Miss Felix say to me one time that I don't need a bunch of fancy clothes or material things for people to notice me, she say that God made me special looking so people would pay close attention to me without all that nonsense.

I think she right, because I get a lot of attention, whether it be good or bad, people notice me when I walk into a room. But today I am nervous to walk into this church room. Nervous that these rich people will see through me right away and know that I am not one of them and maybe even think that I don't belong here. After I stare at my reflection for more than a few seconds, Miss Felix said it was time to go in. I mustered all of the bravery that I had inside of my head, wishing I had snuck Grandma with me, and got out of the car.

As we approached the beautiful building, I was becoming more and more in awe at all of the costumes that everybody was wearing. I mean, I have seen fancy clothes and hats and such things before, but none that I ever seen was like this. It seem like the further we walked into the building, the fancier people got. The mamas and daddies was matching with they kids, and the ladies' hats was like something out of them expensive fashion magazines; hats that looked like they had live animals sitting on top they heads. I swear at one point I saw one lady's hat get up and readjust itself on top of her head. The daddies had on shoes looking like they had done killed off all the gators in the marsh just so they could come to church looking fancy. I wonder how God feel 'bout that? I wonder if God is impressed or saddened by the killing off of all these creatures to look good on a Sunday morning?

I guess that ain't none of my concern, right now all that matter is all these people looking so happy to be here: hugging, and smiling, and holding hands, and singing, and dancing, and smacking on tambourines. When Miss Felix and me walked into that church, I knew we would be leaving as changed women. I just thought we was gonna be leaving together.

6.

Josephine

There is something about summer that drives people wild in the South. I'm not sure if it's the heat or if it's the extra alcohol that the grown folks seem to be drinking because of the heat, but whatever the cause there is something that happens that simply drives everybody crazy. Mother and Father fight extra hard during the summer. They take up screaming and yelling matches more often than they do any other time of the year, and that's saying something because it seems like that's all they do anyway.

I try my best to stay out of their way, usually staying in my room, or taking myself out on walks, or by looking for work during these couple of months off of school. Anything that I can do to just not be around them. I wish that I had more friends. Mother and Father say that friends are nothing but a waste of time at my age. They don't see how I can possibly focus on getting perfect grades in school and manage time for friends in the same lifetime, so they have never really allowed me to hang out with anybody. I guess that's worked out best for me anyway. I don't think that I would have much to talk about with another kid my age. Most thirteen year olds are concerned with playing outside during the summer, running around getting dirty, and things like that. All I want to do is read my books and find a job.

That's why I love working for my Uncle John so much. I've actually worked with him in his bookshop for the past few years during the summer. I help run errands, keep things clean, and organize books and papers—little things like that. He always loves it when I work with him, and I enjoy it too. He is really sweet with me, always praising me and telling me how smart I am, and pretty, and how he wishes he had a baby girl just like me. That always makes me giggle, because I'm black, and my uncle is a white man. He is actually one of my father's oldest friends from when they went to college together, and he has known me all of my life. His wife is very beautiful too. Aunt Susannah was a beauty queen when she was in college, and she has won many competitions for being a real "Southern Belle."

Can you imagine that? Winning a competition just for the way your face and body looks. I mean, I don't see anything wrong with it. I just don't understand how you can give someone a prize for something they didn't create. Heck, if anyone deserves the prize it's God. It's thoughts like these that have been getting me into a lot of trouble lately. Mother has been telling me that it is not a woman's place to have an opinion, and that we were put here on this Earth to be obedient servants, first to God, then to our parents, and then to our husbands. She says that because she was disobedient to her parents and to God, that's why she got stuck with me, and she is going to make damned sure that she raises me to keep my head down, mouth shut, and hands busy. I think she believes that if Father sees me one day, being a good wife and mother, that he will stop hating her for having me, and he will be proud of us both.

Today I have plans to go over to Uncle John's shop to ask him if he would like my help again this summer. I've been waiting for this day since before summer even began. Since the moment the final school bell rang letting us out last week, this is all I've been anticipating. I even picked my outfit out last night, had it pressed, and hung it on the door waiting to be put on. I woke up extra early, gave myself a quick bath, fancied up my hair as best I could, and finally put on that freshly pressed outfit.

After going through every possible thing that I own last night, I decided to wear my prettiest white summer dress with pink and yellow flowers dancing along the shoulder straps and the trim along the bottom. All that's left to do is to put on my white strappy sandals and I'm ready to be on my way. I made sure to leave the house quietly as to not disturb my parents. They probably won't even notice that I'm gone anyway, but just in case they do, last night when I was getting my things ready I wrote a note and left it on the dining table. I figured if they don't find it, at least one of the maids will, just in case someone misses me.

Once outside I embrace the feel of the wind as it grazes along the sides of my cheeks receiving me into its world, begging me to plunge headfirst into my day's adventure. I love the way that summer feels, but even more so the way that summer smells. It smells like heat steaming up from the pavement, like homemade pies sitting out on windowsills to get cool, and sun showers that make people reflect on the things they've done, wondering why God is making it rain on them while the sun is still shining.

I hop on my bicycle and begin my thirty-minute ride to the shop. I can barely contain my pleasure as I pedal, whizzing my way through the light foot traffic and making my way across the only neighborhood I have ever known. I wave to familiar faces, people who do business with my father and shop owners who are now opening their doors for the morning. I enjoy the smells coming from the famous bakery on the corner, tempted to stop and get the first donut fresh off the line. Allowing my mind to wander and roam as freely as I feel, and allowing my feet to pedal furiously and happily. I couldn't wait to get to the shop. I had a feeling this summer was going to change my life.

7.

Thank-You

"Would you like to hold my hand?" the strange lady walking next to me asked. I didn't answer. I barely shook my head in contempt. I was a stranger in a strange land, angry with Miss Felix for deserting me. The cracks on the sidewalk getting bigger with each heavy foot step I took. Why wouldn't she tell me she was bringing me to a new fake mama? Why would she keep that a secret? She ain't never done that before. I ain't never felt so betrayed in my life, and confused. "We don't have a long ways to go now; my house right up the road," the strange lady said, making it obvious that she was trying to be sweet to me. The thoughts in my head swirl all around, conflicting and noisy. On one hand, I didn't want to talk to this new fake mama. I wanted her to know how much disapproval and hurt I felt. On the other hand, she was being real sweet, and it don't seem hardly fair to judge her based on what someone else did.

Before today, I always believed Miss Felix had my best interest at heart, or so I'd hoped. She is always there to protect me, give me advice, and warn me 'bout the dangers in the world. She tell me once that not everybody got good intentions for the nice things they do. She say that some fake daddies might even try to do bad things like touch me in places ain't nobody even ever allowed to see. For a while, I thought I wasn't allowed to see either, so I did all my business looking up at the roof in the bathroom, so God won't think I was bad. One day Miss Felix ask me why I was always complaining about my neck hurting. When I told her what I was doing, she smiled, put her caring hands on my shoulders and explained that I had to look so that I could take proper care of myself, because I don't got a real-life mama to help me do certain lady things.

When the church service ended everyone in the congregation was real friendly. They was all coming up to Miss Felix and me, introducing themselves and they families. Everyone was asking her if I was her daughter, to which she would smile and respond, "If only God would have made me so lucky." After meeting and greeting what felt like everyone in the building, she pulled me off to the side. The look in her eyes giving no warning to what she was 'bout to say. "Thank-You, baby, I gotta tell you something real important. I brought you here for a special purpose today. There's a lady here that I want you to meet." She paused, staring into my eyes trying to gauge my level of understanding before confidently continuing. "Baby girl, you gonna go home with her today. I think that this time gonna be real different than all those other times before. Matter of fact, when I told her yo name was Thank-You she got so filled with joy just to meet you. So how you feel 'bout it sugar? Just temporary to see if y'all blood gonna take a liking to each other?"

In that instance instead of responding, I just stared, fighting back the tears that was welling up in my eyes. I felt like she had done made the decision for me already, so there was no need for me to reply. I stood still, silent, heartbroken at the realization that my most trusted social-worker mama brought me to this big, beautiful place just to set me up. The least she could have done was warn me like she always done in the past. I ain't even bring my favorite things, my picture of Mama, my dolls, nothing. I thought Miss Felix ain't got no good intentions like all them bad people she warn me 'bout. After she introduced me to my new fake mama, she gave me a hug and said her goodbyes. I sat by the big, ole window inside the church, the one that people use to look into so they can witness the holiness that be going on inside, and me and all my goose pimples sat and watched as she drove away.

"Here we is, baby girl. Home sweet home." I look up at the house we are approaching, my eyes growing wider. "It's beautiful," I mutter, breaking the long held silence. I was unable to blink, as my eyes breathed in the beauty that stood before it. The house wasn't as large as some of the other houses we passed by along our path, but it stole my breath. The grass was perfectly green, the kind of green that make you think of picnics and playing. The flowers lining the walkway to the front porch were as yellow as the sun, shining rays of happiness into my eyes and into the eyes of all who pass by. Beauty is an amazing thing. It's like a spirit taking ownership over what it's possessin', taking ownership over my thoughts. As we continued our walk to the front door, I noticed the porch, each plank settled perfectly in its place, serving as a base for what appeared to be the oldest rocking chair I have ever seen.

All of a sudden the reality of the situation began to come into focus, causing a sensation of guilt to sweep across my mind. The need to apologize to my new fake mama becoming more and more apparent. She was probably just as afraid as I was. Before I was able to get my apologies out, she looked down at me, stopping in front of the pretty white front doors. "Thank-You, I know you is scared, baby girl, cuz you don't know me. Truthfully, I'm scared too. But, if you give me a chance to be a good mama, maybe we won't ever have to be afraid again, or alone." With her words, every negative emotion that was seeking a home inside my heart and mind was no longer welcome. I looked my new fake mama square in her face and showed her how much my teeth love to feel the wind.

8.

Josephine

I must have been more excited than I realized to get to my destination. My feet pedaled faster than I have ever pedaled before, almost losing a sandal in the process. A bike ride that should have taken me thirty minutes, only took me seventeen. I was so early, Uncle John wasn't even there yet. Luckily for me I absolutely love the part of town that his bookshop is in. It is right in the middle of a beautiful cobblestone-lined street, surrounded by small cafes, restaurants, and little shops that sell knickknacks and things. Things that Mother says are a waste of time and money. If it was later in the day, perhaps I would have gone into some of those other shops, but it was too early and everybody was now opening up and getting their things organized for the long and beautiful day ahead of them.

Instead I decided to take a seat on the stoop, wait patiently, and take in life as it unfolded before me. It's always so interesting watching how people live, watching how they walk, how they talk, and interact with each other. There are some things that you simply can't learn in school. You can only learn by keeping your eyes open to the world that's opening up right in front of your eyes. In the back of my mind, excitement lingered at the thought of seeing my uncle, and discovering what new things the shop would have in store for me this summer, assuming that is, that I get the job.

I can't even imagine what I would do if I don't get it. I mean, I hadn't even really thought about it, because I've gotten it for the past few summers. But what if Uncle John just doesn't need the help anymore, or what if he already has somebody else, somebody older, prettier, or smarter? It's not only that I love my uncle or that working for him is fun, I mainly love working here because he owns a bookshop. And not just any old bookshop. He owns one of the oldest bookshops in this part of the South.

Like my father inherited his money, Uncle John inherited his books, actually the whole store has been passed down in his family for generations. He sells all kinds of glorious books, and I don't just say that because books are probably my most favorite things ever, after Aunt Clara's pecan pie, I say that because he gets praises from all types of folks for his wide variety and collection of books. He has even won some awards. If I don't get this job, where on earth am I going to find free books to read all summer? I can't go to the library, because the library in our town is named after Father's family and Mother often spends a lot of her time there handling charities, community events, and other things—which she says I have no business knowing about. She doesn't ever let me go there with her. She would never let me be seen with my face buried in books, that according to her, serve no real purpose in life.

As I sit on the stoop getting nervous about the possibility of not being able to get free books to read all summer, Uncle John pulls up in his beat-up, old, red pickup truck. I swear that thing is so old one would imagine he could retire it into some kind of truck museum, or something like that. I like that about him though, everybody in town knows that Uncle John has lots of money. I don't think Father would still be friends with him if he didn't, but he doesn't mind driving around town in his old truck, waving, honking his horn, and smiling at everybody as he drives by.

As soon as he parked, and hopped out of the truck, he saw me and gave me the biggest smile I have ever seen anybody give in my life. I didn't even know smiles could be so big. It looked like his mouth was stretching so wide it was ready to touch his ears from tip to tip. I think my uncle is really handsome. In fact, if I could, I would take him to school for show and tell. He's kind of stocky with muscles much bigger than Fathers, dark blue eyes that make you feel like you're staring into the deepest parts of the ocean, and the most beautiful thick curly blonde hair I have ever seen growing on a human.

"Is that my little honey dew, looking so beautiful and grown-up?" The sound of his voice causing my excitement to come alive. "Hi, Uncle John," I say as I run over and jump into his arms. "My goodness, girl, what have you been eating all year? You're as heavy as a sack of marbles that's been soaked in the rain!" We both giggled as he put me down. I figured he knew why I was here, so I didn't bother mentioning anything right away. Instead, I followed him into the shop.

As soon as he opened up the doors the wonderful smell of books hit the tips of my scent receptors, causing my eyes to fill with tears as I was surrounded by a feeling so comforting. Uncle

John looked down at me with a similar look in his eyes. I think anyone that truly loves words and books would bond in a building where books are the center of attention. A bookshop is a like a church, except in a bookshop the books are God, and all who enter those doors, come to worship them. "So you ready to work, honey dew?"

"Of course I am, sir. When can I get started?" We both laughed again, and all of my nervous energy crept as quietly out of my mind as it entered.

9.

Thank-You

Miss Clara is real pretty. Looking like she could have been a movie star back in her day. She 'bout the same age as Miss Felix, except real tall and thin. Skin the perfect mixture between chocolate and bronze, and so silky she ain't never gotta wear no makeup. Her hair is the color of nutmeg that reach quite down the middle of her back. When we go to that big fancy church every Sunday, everybody know her, and she so friendly with all them people. She be knowing all they names, and she be asking 'bout every one of they family members. "How yo mama, yo daddy, yo cousins, they kids?" The best part is when she introduce me to people and she say, "This my baby Thank-You; ain't she the prettiest thing you ever seen?" Ain't nobody never claimed me like that before, calling me theirs. She make me feel so special. She don't let nobody treat me no different, as if I didn't belong. She even took me shopping and got me a bunch of new clothes, and when I say new, I mean brand new from the store. I ain't never put something on that ain't been worn by somebody before me.

Life these past few weeks with her have been wonderful. We're learning all 'bout each other. She ain't never been married or never had no kids of her own, but she tell me stories all the time of when she was a little girl, and how life was like when she grew up. When she tell me 'bout them stories her eyes change, like part of her still living in them memories. She ran away from home when she was thirteen and lived off the streets till she was nineteen, because she ain't wanna follow her mama and daddy rules. By the time she was ready to come home and ask for forgiveness, both her parents had died leaving her with enough money to live off of, a big beautiful fancy house, and a hole in her heart so big she could fit the whole world inside it. She say since then she learned to appreciate everything 'bout life. That's why she take a liking to me before she even met me, because Miss Felix tell her my name was "Thank-You."

Today is our first home visit with Miss Felix. That's when she come by to inspect my new fake mamas and daddies to see how they treating me. When she arrived I was expecting her to be how she normally is on these home visits. She usually real formal, notepad in her hand, glasses sitting on the tip of her nose, and her pen don't stop writing things down. She also don't ever take no food anybody offer her. But not here, not with Miss Clara. "Clara, I cannot say no to your pecan pie," she said with a greedy look in her eyes. We all sat at the table as Miss Clara served some of the best homemade pecan pie I have ever tasted. "This pie so good, you know it brushed the lips of God, once or twice," Miss Felix say to my fake mama. "Woooo weeeee, Clara, you know I love it when you make this pie!"

I sat listening to them talk, trying to piece together parts of they conversation. It's real strange listening to the way they speak to each other. They acting like they been knowing each other since the beginning of time. I don't want them to know that I'm being as nosy as a snout on a pig, so I stare at my pie, taking small little bites, even though I wanna shove the whole dang thing in my mouth. As sly as I thought I was being, Miss Felix know me all too well. In the middle of her conversation she stopped talking and looked directly at me. "Baby girl, you wanna know what we talking 'bout, cuz yo pie ain't barely moving off of that plate, less you don't like it?" I look up, knowing my teeth ain't willing to sacrifice this delicious pecan pie to tell a lie. Forced into the truth, I nodded my head, acknowledging that I want to be informed.

Miss Felix and Miss Clara took the next hour to tell me all about the history of their friendship. Stopping only to smile, laugh, or cry along the way. As the story goes, they met when they was both sixteen years old. That's around the time when Miss Clara was living off the streets and staying in different shelters. As fate would have it, at that same time Miss Felix was volunteering after school in the very same shelters. Miss Felix said at first they couldn't stand each other, because she grew up dirt poor, yet she pushed herself to get an education and to stay out of trouble, while Miss Clara was born with privilege, and money, yet she ain't have no appreciation for nothing or nobody.

Miss Clara said it took them a couple years and a couple of arguments before they reached a place of understanding. Instead of yelling at each other, they began to listen to each other. It was then that they began to forge a decades-long bond. Before they knew it, they was the best of friends. Miss Felix is actually one of the reasons Miss Clara stopped acting a fool and decided to change her life and come home. By the time the story was finished, they were both holding hands, tears in their eyes, and smiles on their faces. Gratitude resonating across the table, touching my heart so deeply I began to cry and smile with them.

Miss Felix thought it was best to not tell me nothing about their friendship, or even give me a hint that very first Sunday, because she ain't want none of us getting in no trouble with the state. According to her social-worker mama rules, she ain't allowed to get too personal with her orphaned kids. But, she say I'm special. After the last fake mama said she ain't want me no more, Miss Felix decided she was gonna do everything in her power to see to it that I found the perfect home. She promised herself that she would find me a family that would love me for me and not try to parade me around like some kind of charity case, or point out my differences. That's when she thought about Miss Clara, because if she know anybody in this whole wide world that don't judge nobody, and just love everybody for who they is, it's Miss Clara. So, here we is, trying it out for the summer. Miss Clara with me, and me with Miss Clara.

After she left, my new fake mama and me cleaned up all the dirty dishes. I like that she don't make me do everything. We work together to keep the house tidy and to fix meals. As we was cleaning the kitchen, we was talking, telling jokes, stories, and secrets. She told me 'bout the potions she make for people, saying that one day she gonna show me how to make them too. I was happy to be included in every part of her world.

Right before we finished up, Miss Clara stopped working, looked over at me and put her rag down. I could almost see the thoughts formulating in her mind behind her molasses-colored eyes. She was silent for a few moments, before finally speaking. "Thank-You, baby, how you feel 'bout coming with me to the library next week? I volunteer there for the summer, teaching folks how to do crafts and things. You can come with me if you want?" Well, I been knowing that Miss Clara like to read, because she got a lot of books all over her big fancy house. She got books in every bedroom, in the den, and she even got books sitting up right next to the toilet in all the bathrooms, so it's no surprise to me that's where she decided to volunteer her time.

Nervously, I looked up at my fake mama. I wanted to go more than I wanted another piece of that wonderful pecan pie, but sometimes new things can be downright scary, and I don't know if my teeth gonna like the library as much as they liked that pie. Feeling those little familiar goose pimples start creeping their way through the surface of my skin, I clear my throat, take a deep breath, and without much confidence shared with Miss Clara my biggest secret. "I would love to go with you, and thank you for wanting to take me. But, Miss Clara, ma'am, I don't know how to read." Instead of saying a word, she walked right on up to me and gave me a hug. My new fake mama stood in the kitchen and held me. She held me like a real-life mama would hold her real-life baby, and I swear I could almost feel them big ole holes in both of our hearts get a little bit smaller.

10.

Josephine

There is nothing better than being able to swim in a pool of knowledge so deep it forces ignorance to be uncomfortable in its own skin, to where it no longer holds a sense of being, a sense of purpose. That's what books do. They allow us to live in the minds of every type of human. They allow us to taste the kind of freedom that even the end of slavery didn't bring. Here in the South we deal with ignorance every day. Some days it's not so obvious, and some days it feels like ignorance can walk right up and slap you in the face. Especially working here in the bookshop with Uncle John. No matter how much money my family has, or how good of an education I get, they still want to know why this white man has himself a little Negro girl working here.

I know Uncle John lost a lot of customers because of me. He has never told me, but I've watched them all as they come and go. I've watched their reactions as they blatantly stare at me, unsure if they are daring me to flinch, or to bow? I'll never know which, because I'm yet to do either. I am so grateful because Uncle John really cares for me, so much so he's willing to lose business just to keep me around. I make it up to him by doing all that I can around here. I answer the phones if they ring, I sweep up, I organize his files, and I keep the books in as much order as I can; which gets a bit tough since I'm not allowed to climb up on the big ladder by myself. I can only fix the top shelf if Uncle John is holding the bottom of the ladder, ready to catch me if I fall.

I like working here so much it seems as if my days go by like a whirlwind. The only way that I can keep time balanced is by finding new and old books to read. It's great that Uncle John lets me take books home as long as I'm super careful with them, that way when I'm done reading them I can bring them back to the shop. And if I fall in love with one, then I pay for it out of my weekly pay and take it home to live with me. I don't even bother asking Mother and Father for the money, because they think the only books worth reading are schoolbooks. They say that imaginations are for fools and for poor people that don't have anything better to do with their time. My parents remind me of the people that give me those mean looks, sometimes when I look at their faces, they look just like them. Ignorance may be possessed by many, but it has only one face.

Today I have a lot to do in the shop. I have so many errands to run, files to organize, shelves to dust. Uncle John is so proud of all the hard work that I've been doing. The past few summers that I've worked here I only worked for a few hours each day, but this summer he talked to my parents and asked if I could stay and work for just about the whole day, since I'm older now and much more responsible. I know my parents don't care two nickels what I do with my day, as long as I'm not in their way, so they gave Uncle John the permission to keep me around the shop as long as he needs me.

I think it's great. I get to be around books all day, and be around somebody who actually appreciates my presence. There is even a new book I found that I can't wait to take home. It's about a little girl that becomes friends with animals on a big farm; her best friend is even a little pig. I asked Uncle John if he would keep it under the counter for me until I get paid, so that I can buy it. I already know that I'm going to love it.

The only thing that I don't like about working here these longer hours is that Uncle John isn't really here as much as I thought he would be. By about lunch time he is already packing up his stuff to head out, and most days he doesn't come back until really late in the afternoon, which is fine as long as he's back in time for me to ride my bike home before it gets dark. Some of those days he even comes in here smelling the way most grownups smell in the summer. He smells like dirt, sweat, and sour liquor.

11.

Thank-You

I'm so nervous; I don't think I slept a wink of sleep last night. See, everybody got something they 'fraid of. I don't care who you is, how brave you is, or where you come from. That's just a simple truth we human beans got in common—after love, we share fear. But the thing 'bout them two things is, they can never survive in the same space together. You can never learn to love something if you fear it. It ain't complicated reasoning. Grown folks got they heads wrapped round all kinds of things to be 'fraid of. That's why hate exist in this world, and that's where it come from.

Today is the day I'm gonna conquer my fear. I'm going with Miss Clara to the town library, and I'm gonna learn me how to read. I'm real excited, but I'm real scared too. I always like how pretty books look, all the color pictures they got on the covers inviting you to peek inside. I like how they smell, comforting in some strange way, almost familiar. In my head when I think of reading books, I think of going to dinner at somebody house with Miss Clara and I get to try all kinds of new foods, foods that I done smelled before but ain't never tasted. That's how books make me feel, like I can eat them up and either love how they taste, or just wanna spit them right back on out. The only difference between reading and eating is I know how to eat because my teeth like food, but I think something wrong with my eyes. It's not that I can't see good, because I see real good. I just think that my eyes seen so much bad in the world they don't wanna help me see what's inside of no books, in case we find more bad. That's where my fear come from.

Even with all that I find myself thinking about words a lot. I know that might sound silly coming from a somebody that don't know how to read, but I love words something serious, just not in a way that most people love them. I can't use them to read sentences, or I can't say that I love how to spell them, because I can't spell too good, but I love how words can affect the people we choose to speak them to. Miss Felix, my social-worker mama, used to tell me that words is one of the most powerful things on the face of this earth. "Words can be used as a weapon for good or for evil, baby. They could build us up or break us down. If when we speak, we choose only words that build rather than break, then we can change the world around us, and maybe one day even change the whole world."

She would say my real-life mama must have known that because of my name. Because she knew that everybody would always find a reason to give thanks around me, and when people is grateful for things that's when all the blessings come their way. She said since she been my social-worker mama she been blessed so much, and all she gotta do is call out my name. I like when she tell me stuff like that because it feel nice. But ain't that what words is for, to have a way to share with people how they make you feel on the inside to build them up like Miss Felix say. Some people say it's so we could talk to God, but I don't think that's it. I think since God could hear all our thoughts anyway, He or She don't need no more compliments, no sweet sugar talk, so we just wasting all them good words sucking up to a God that we don't even gotta suck up to. I think God gave us words so we could use them on each other, because humans don't read minds like God do. Except it seem like all people do is save all the good words for those moments when they praying out loud, so they sound real pretty, and when they done praying they cussing out their neighbor with all the other words they got left over.

Maybe I'm too young to do anything about all that, or maybe not. But my purpose for today ain't to change the world. Today, I'm gonna learn me how to read. Miss Clara say when we go to the library, she gonna set me up with someone real kind that work there that teach people with scared eyes like mine how to read. She say that my eyes don't gotta be afraid no more, because sometimes in life you can't pick the good and the bad moments that are put in front of you, but with books, you can always choose what you set your eyes to see. "You ready, baby girl?" I hear Miss Clara say as she walking up behind me. "As ready as I'll ever be, ma'am." With those words out of my mouth we made our way out of the house, holding hands as we got onto the sidewalk.

The walk to the library is a short one. Miss Clara don't like to drive her car if she don't need to. She say that cars is an easy way to get lazy, and our ancestors ain't know nothing 'bout no cars. She said by not using the car often, you have to make a conscious decision about everywhere you want to be putting yourself. If you really want to be somewhere, then it's worth the walk, and if it ain't, then you best not go. She say by practicing thinking like this I can set myself up for a life of making good decisions. She also say she want me to learn the path real well, that way if I ever want to go to the library by myself I could find it with no problem. I love to walk anyway, and walking with Miss Clara is fun because she so much like me. She like to point out beautiful things, like bumble bees, wild herbs and flowers growing along fences, tangling their way into a beautiful weave of graceful chaos. She even take a plastic bag with us too so we can pick up trash lazy people throw on the sidewalk.

We been walking everywhere since I got here. I think I'm becoming familiar with the way the neighborhood is laid out. There are always people waving and saying hello to each other, pies of all sorts, each with their own delicious scent cooling on the windowsills of some of the prettiest houses I have ever seen, and grass so perfectly green it make you appreciate every single blade, thanking them for coming together the way they do. As we get closer to the library, I could feel the excitement brewing in Miss Clara, "You ready, baby? The knowledge that this building hold gonna change your life, you'll see." All I could do was hold on to her hand tighter, and anticipate all that was to come.

12.

Josephine

It's awfully lonely in the bookshop once the sun starts to go down. Uncle John is usually here by now, but it seems like the sky is growing as dark as my imagination, and I'm wondering if something terrible has happened to him. I didn't even realize how late it was getting until I noticed my shadow begin to dim with the exiting of the sun. When the sun is up and high in the sky as it can get, I have my shadow to keep me company, but at night I feel like there are other shadows around, ones that are not friendly at all. I'm not saying that I believe in ghosts, although I am old enough to read ghost stories if I wanted to. I'm saying that there is something about nighttime that unsettles my spirit, especially here, alone in the bookshop.

I busied myself with all the tasks that I had to complete today. I was able to finish all the work that I needed to get done, and was even able to do some extra organizing and dusting so that my load tomorrow would be much lighter. I walked around the bookshop, making my way up and down the aisles a few times before deciding that worrying had never done anything good for anybody. It was time that I took the initiative to keep myself calm and safe. So I made the decision to lock all of the doors in the shop, get a comfy spot on the ground, and read until Uncle John came back, hoping that it would be soon and wondering if he would be able to carry me home tonight. I've never ridden my bicycle this late before. I walked over to the front door of the shop and flipped the "OPEN" sign to "CLOSED," turning the deadbolt on the door to its locked position.

My mind was beginning to race again. Worry has a way of creeping in and out of open windows and doors unless they are fastened tightly. My mind willing Uncle John to hurry, yet hoping that no one else was going to come by wanting to purchase any books. Considering I've never stayed here this late, I really have no idea what time the shop stays open for its regular customers. But, I figure if anyone knocks on the glass, I would hide until they walked away, that way no one would know that I was alone in the shop, and afraid.

Once every door and window was tightly locked, and everything from the day's work put away in their respective places, I made my way around the counter. That's where Uncle John usually keeps the books that people put on reserve. Sure enough, there was my book, sitting real pretty on top of the pile. *Charlotte's Web*, it's called, and I think I'm just going to love everything about this book. Maybe even by reading it I'll figure a way to convince Mother and Father into buying me a few animals of my own. They don't see the purpose in keeping pets, which is no surprise. They barely see the purpose in keeping me.

With the book in my hand, and my comfy spot on the ground, I settled in to read and to wait, hoping that Uncle John comes soon so that the shadows don't interfere with me. The first page of *Charlotte's Web* had me hooked. The very first page reminded me a bit of my own life, and immediately I felt a connection to Wilbur. I can't believe that the farmer wanted to kill him just because he is different than the other pigs. I eagerly filled my eyes with the beautiful words and images that lined the beginning pages of my new favorite book, reading slowly as I didn't want to miss a single breath, a single comma, or a single emotion. I read until my eyes began to feel heavy.

I must have fallen asleep thinking on my own experiences and how my life related to that of Wilbur, the pig. My dreams were vivid, alive with thoughts of living my life peacefully and happily on a farm. I was sleeping soundly until the sound of footsteps coming from the back of the bookshop suddenly stunned me awake. I stayed still as a beetle lying on the ground with my eyes closed tight, praying that it was Uncle John coming in through the back door. *But why the back?* I think to myself. He has a key for the front.

My nerves were racing up and down under my skin, through my chest, and into my belly. I couldn't even comprehend how long I'd been asleep for, or if my parents were worried about me, or how I would defend myself if it were a robber. I felt every breath as it entered and exited my body, slow and shallow, telling myself to keep as calm as possible, and to be brave if I needed to be. Uncle John would be proud of me if someone was breaking in and I stopped them. My mother and father would be proud too. They would be so grateful that their little, brave girl was able to fend off robbers, and then they would realize how much they loved me after all. I would be a hero.

As nice as all that sounded, and as brave as I wanted to be, I was frozen. The footsteps drew nearer, and I felt the presence of a shadow—one that did not come here to be my friend. My spirit knew it, and was giving my mind all the signals that it needed to propel me to get up and to run, to run as fast as I could. But I was still frozen. As the shadow grew luminously closer, my body started to tremble. I felt goose bumps emerge out of the depths of my skin and immediately begin racing up and down my arms and legs. My jaw locked as I tried everything in my power to not cry. Whoever owned this shadow was now standing over me.

I lay wondering if they would kill a little girl like me, because here in the South I've heard many stories of little, black girls like me being killed. There was a story I heard once about four little girls like me even dying inside of a church, because an ignorant man decided to play God and firebomb the church they were in. If the real God wasn't able to protect those little girls, how can He protect me? I always wondered about that, what that must have felt like for them? Going to a place where you should feel the safest, a place where you expect God to protect you, and you never walk out alive. My Sunday school teacher says that God chose those girls because Heaven needed some more angels. Because when you die at the hand of something so evil God reserves a special place for you. Tonight, I would be jealous of those girls because they got the death that I could only pray for. They got the special reservation in Heaven that I was not so lucky to receive.

I felt the shadow touch my face, at this point my tears were flowing without my permission. I tried to hold them in, but my fear was uncontrollable. The shadow knelt down beside me, and I could feel its breath close to my face, hot and steady. I didn't have the sense to open my eyes. I didn't have the sense to scream, all I could do was lie there. I thought that if God wanted to make me an angel, surely there was a better way to go about it than this.

This shadow made me feel ashamed of myself, ashamed that I wasn't fighting back, ashamed that I was never going to make Mother and Father proud of me. As its hands went up my dress, I yelped, angry with myself for not doing more. Why couldn't I do more?

The shadow put its entire weight on top of me. At this point I was flat on my back, unable to take a full breath. My sobs uncontrollable and using up every ounce of air I gasped for. Its hand was now over my mouth, suffocating the noise of my silent screams, as its other hand struggled to unzip its pants. I could feel its frustration. I could feel its bravery that smothered my own, and eventually after what felt like an eternity of struggling and repositioning itself on top of me, I felt it enter the part of my body that Mother said was for my husband and my husband only. I screamed out in pain. I screamed out in anger. I screamed out in disappointment. I screamed out in embarrassment. I screamed out for every little girl whose innocence was murdered, leaving yet again another breathing corpse. It was then that I smelled it; the scent that was once comforting, and familiar. The shadow smelled of dirt, sweat, and sour liquor.

61

13.

Thank-You

"Magical." That's the only word that can manage to escape from my mind, slipping quietly out my mouth as we walk into the The Dieu Foundation Family Library. I would have never imagined, even in my wildest dreams, that a building could be this beautiful. "Miss Clara, you sure we in the library, ma'am?" I say in a daze. I hear her chuckle, as her hand squeezes a bit more tightly round mine.

I felt almost out of breath, giddy with excitement and over-whelmed that a building that was built by human hands could look as if it fell straight outta Heaven. The ceilings was so high they was almost touching the clouds. There's more than one level. I counted at least three, with a grand staircase right in the middle of the building that lead people like me straight up into them clouds. Paintings of all kinds decorate the walls, engraving images into my mind of things that I ain't never seen before, but will surely now dream 'bout. Chubby-cheeked babies flying round with arrows stare back at me, recognizing my presence. Stern-faced women dressed in long flowing gowns stand next to visibly proud men with strange black hats sitting high up on they heads. "Miss Clara, who all the people in these paintings?" I ask, my mind fresh with theories of my own.

"You okay, baby girl? Don't wander too far now." I hear Miss Clara's voice coming from somewhere around me. She must not have heard my question. I didn't even realize when our hands let go of each other. I was in a moment of perpetual wonderment, amazement, reverence, whatever the fancy word be to describe standing in a place unlike any place you ever been in your life. It left me wondering how I could change the life of someone else in the same way that walking into this place changed mine.

I walked into that library and felt like every piece of my soul belonged there. Being around all these books make me feel alive in a way I ain't never felt before. And for the first time, I wasn't scared to see what was in books. I was excited at the thought of my world expanding so large, my mind wouldn't be able to contain it. "Miss Clara?" I say, looking around to see where she is. I spot her talking to an older man standing behind a high wooden desk, that desk looking like it made from one hundred oak trees, beautiful for what it is, an eternal coffin.

I make my way over to Miss Clara, she standing there tall and sleek carrying on a lively conversation with the man. He clearly got teeth that must really like Miss Clara, cuz all they doing is showing themselves. That man showing so much teeth, my own teeth getting a bit jealous. He real tall like my new fake mama, not as dark but his skin just as nice. He dress real sharp; not as fancy as he going to church, but he keep himself clean and nice.

"Clarence, this here my baby girl, Thank-You," Miss Clara say as she noticed me approaching. He look over at me; his expression showing a bit of incomprehension. "Well, Clara, I didn't know you had yourself a little one. Good morning, beautiful. It's nice to meet you. But, I'm so sorry I didn't catch your name?" Miss Clara look over at him giving him a quick and a firm response, "It's Thank-You. Her name is Thank-You."

I get that a lot, people asking me to repeat my name cuz they ain't never catch it the first time. It's just something my new fake mama gotta get used to. Sometimes I think people hear it, but they so taken aback that somebody got a name they ain't used to hearing, so they make them repeat it. I don't mind it, not one bit. Like Miss Felix say, I get to remind people to be grateful all the time.

"So what brings you into our library today, Miss Thank-You?" Mister Clarence say, teeth still showing. I took a second before giving my answer, allowing my bravery to show its face. "Well, sir, I come in today with my Miss Clara, cuz I gonna learn how to read, so I could read every book you got." With that Mister Clarence clapped his hands together and replied, "Well let's get started then. You have a lot of work to do if you're to read all of the books we have here. How would you like a personal tour of the entire library before we get you reading?" He looked so excited that I was now discovering this new wonderful world. I couldn't resist the thought of getting a personal tour. "Sounds great to me," I replied happily.

Miss Clara wasn't able to join us cuz she had to get started on her volunteering for the day. She come here so she can teach people how to do different crafts. She so good at making things, she got herself a line of people waiting to sit in on her class. One of the best things 'bout the library besides how big and beautiful it is, is that everything is free. All the books is free to read. You can even take them home long as you return them when you done, and all they classes is free too. Ain't nobody got to pay to go to Miss Clara class. She do it cuz she say she love helping people, and ain't nothing in the world like teaching people how to do something they ain't never done before.

"Let's go, little one, I have a nametag written out for you. You are my honorary helper today and any other day. Whenever you'd like. When you are here with your Miss Clara, and your reading session is over, you can hang with me and run the library." I was fit as a peach, I ain't never had no kind of job before, and I ain't never had a sticker with my name on it so everybody could see. I placed my sticker right underneath my chin and a little over to the right. It just felt like the perfect spot. With "My Name Is Thank-You" written across my heart, we were ready to start.

We began our tour of the library on the first floor, that's where Mister Clarence say all the magic happens. Off to the far back left, they have the "Kids Reading Corner," that's where I'm gonna learn how to read. On the far back right that's where Miss Clara teaching her craft class, many other classes happen back there too. They call that the "Culture Corner." As we walking around taking in the beautiful sights learning my way around, Mister Clarence begin explaining to me the history of the library.

The building is over two hundred years old, and was once a home occupied by one of the wealthiest families in this part of the South. That's actually where the library got its name. When the Dieu family donated this house to the town, the leaders thought it fit to name such a charitable contribution after the family that contributed it, calling it The Dieu Foundation Family Library. He say this family got so much money they last name actually mean "God." I ain't never heard nothing like that in my life. "Mister Clarence, it seem like they thought of themselves something extra special." He nodded in agreement, and we continued our walk.

"So where they living now?" I ask, enjoying the tour but unable to get the story of this family out of my mind. "Who?" he replied looking a bit puzzled. Before I could clarify my question, he remembered our conversation and continued talking. "Oh yes, the Dieu's. I think they are living in a house off of Juniper Trace. Do you know where that is? It's not too far from your Miss Clara's house." I honestly don't know my way around the neighborhood yet, but something about this family making me curious to find out more. I ain't never been a nosy kind of kid. I think everybody business is they own business, and that's that. So why is my mind racing at the thought of finding out more?

"Are they nice people?" I ask. I watched him as he thought about my question for a moment. The creases on his forehead tightened and scrunched together as he stood, tracing all of the paths in his mind that may lead him to a memory of an encounter with any of them. "Mrs. Dieu used to come in here all the time, many years back. I was only a volunteer here then, so she never spoke to me, but I would see her all of the time. You can ask your Miss Clara. She would know more than I do. All I know for certain is they had a death in the family. Since then no one really sees them." The word "death" always brings my spirit to a halt. It's a word that has visited my dreams. It's the word that has me here today. Death is not the reason for my life, but it is the reason for my life story. Without death, I would not be an orphan named Thank-You, getting ready to learn to read in this big, beautiful, magical world filled with books. Without death, I don't know who I would be. As we continued our tour through the library, it became harder and harder to focus, my thoughts drowning out Mister Clarence's voice. My search for knowledge was quickly evolving into something more.

PART TWO

Fall

14.

Josephine

The weather is beginning to change. I lay in bed peeking out from under my covers, the sunlight barely making its way into the creases that I call my eyes. I can see the trees outside of my window, the way the wind rustles the leaves as their colors begin to change from bright green to a rusty shade of orange. All year I look forward to when I get to witness the leaves as they evolve. Watching as they dance around in the freedom of the wind, disembarking from their temporary tree branch home. Grateful that I get to witness their fall, landing softly on the ground, continuing the cycle that we call life.

I miss the feel of the wind. Closing my eyes again, I wished that I were one of those leaves, able to disembark from my body and dance freely into the wind. Turning into soil so that my life would not have been a waste but a blessing. Adding to the richness of a newly birthed plant, or adding years to a tree that has witnessed as many years as the earth. The same earth that it ripped through to stand higher upon the ground. I grip my covers tighter. I can't keep my eyes closed for too long anymore, without remembering.

"Josephine," I hear my mother screaming my name from the bottom of the stairs. She has been trying to get me to leave my room for almost two months, and now that school has started I may not be able to hide in here forever. I hear her heavy footsteps as they barrel up the stairs. She is either still drunk from last night or starting her day off like she normally does with a special kick added to her coffee. "Josephine," I hear her screaming now from outside of my door, her voice piercing through my walls, and my ears. "Josephine, you stupid child, I don't care if you want to sleep until you're dead, but you are either going to go to school or live out on the street where you belong."

It's sad, when you are so used to the viciousness in a person's voice, that it no longer causes an effect. Your heart no longer hurts, and that rippling pain that one feels throughout their body when being screamed at, or confronted, no longer exists. I continue to lie in bed, shutting my eyes tighter, eventually pulling the covers over my head, shutting out all sights, sounds, and smells of the world that exists outside of my cocoon. In here I am safe. I am safe from my parents. I am safe from the shadows that do not belong to me.

"Josephine, if you're not sitting outside waiting for that school bus again, I swear I'm going to have Father get someone to bust your door down. Everybody at the charity auction last night wanted to know why Josephine wasn't in school all last week? You think I give a damn that you want to be an uneducated street-walker? These people are my friends, and they are very generous when donating to our charities. I'm sick and tired of you making us look like fools. If you were a boy you would have had more common sense."

She yells, she hollers, she says, "If you were a boy." I've been hearing her repeat those words all of my life. And every time they enter my ears my heart grows a bit colder to the God that created me opposite of what was needed and wanted around here. If I were a boy, I wouldn't be afraid of anything, or of anyone. I would be safe from evil hands that grope and roam. I would have no reason to be ashamed of my body or myself. I would never feel dirty, because I would be the one in control, and I would never use my strength to hurt anything smaller than me.

I want to scream at God the way my mother screams at me. I want to march up to the gates of Heaven and kick my feet into the door as she does my bedroom. "God, get out here. Show your face, you coward. You have the whole world believing that you exist, and you're nothing but a lying coward. You promise people salvation yet you can't save them from anything; you couldn't even save me. Why didn't you save me you coward?"

I replayed that conversation in my mind, sobbing into my pillow with a force so tremendous I thought my lungs were going to make their way up my throat and out of my mouth, exposing all of the air that I had inside of my body to the air that exists on the outside. I sobbed until I fell back asleep. Wrapped in the warmth of sadness, I sleep, I dream, I wake up screaming. Then, I sleep again. That is the tally of my days; what my existence has become because I was not born a boy.

15.

Thank-You

"'S-o I li-ived my li-fe a-lone, wi-ith-out any-one t-hat I c-ou-ld re-aally talk to.' How was that, ma'am?" I look up proudly from my book *The Little Prince* at Miss Felix. She was staring down at me so proud, like I was her own baby showing her I could read for the first time. I ain't see her in almost a whole entire month, and the last time she was here, I wasn't ready to show her the progress I was making. I was too scared. "Thank-You, baby, I am so proud of you. You doing such a good job, you gonna be able to teach me how to read all them fancy books you reading." I giggle, I know Miss Felix could read real good—she ain't the smartest person I ever met for nothing.

"So, baby, your reading got so much better over the summer. I am so happy you got over your fear of looking in them books and stuck this through. As much as I love listening to you read though, baby girl, you know I'm here for an important visit. It's time we make some big decisions." I say okay, nodding slowly, scared that she's about to tell me that Miss Clara don't want me no more. "Miss Felix, ma'am, is you gonna take me back to the home?" The anticipation was killing my nerves on the inside. I had to know.

"What you think you want to happen, baby girl?" Well Miss Felix ain't never ask me before what I want, or who I want to stay with. I mean, ain't nobody ever been really fit to keep me anyway, but this the first time she actually wanting to know what I think. Maybe she thinking I'm much smarter now that I can read so good. "Ma'am, if it was up to me, I would want my real-life mama to be alive, but since I can't get that I'm happy being anywhere you think it's best to put me. But just so you know, I love Miss Clara. She treat me real nice. She always encouraging me to do better, to read them fancy books, to think for myself and to use wisdom. She make the best dang pecan pie I ever tasted in my entire life, and she always telling me she love me." She listened intently, jotting down my words as I was speaking them. Her black blazer speckled with tiny white dots of fuzz and lint, cascading a size too big over her broad shoulders.

"Is that all, Thank-You?" she say, still staring down at her notebook. I mean, I can't think of nothing else to tell Miss Felix that she don't already know 'bout Miss Clara. They still the best of friends. "No, ma'am, that's all. I ain't sure what else I can say. It really up to Miss Clara now, ain't it?" She looked at me and nodded as she stood up, not showing any signs of emotion as she excused herself to go speak with Miss Clara. She was waiting on the front porch swaying back and forth in the rocking chair that been passed down in her family for generations. She tell me that rocking chair been sitting on that porch as long as this house been here.

I sat alone in the sitting room, wondering what it must feel like to be a part of something for so long. To be a blessing to everyone who come in contact with you. That's what that rocking chair is, a blessing. It heal weary feet, put hollering babies to sleep, soothe the sadness in many souls. I wish my life's purpose could be like that, so that when my last breath leave my body, I know that I done lived it well. Miss Clara say that I got a special kind of soul, that it ain't as young as my age make it seem. She say my soul old, like it done been recycled a few times in other bodies, and other lives. I always find it interesting when she say that, to think there was other versions of Thank-You walking this earth before I was even a thought, or "a glimmer in my daddy eye," like she say.

They was out there for a good while, at least twenty minutes before I heard the croak of the heavy front door as it opened slowly. I listened to the shuffling of they feet as they made their way over to the sitting area where Miss Felix left me. I look down at the palm of my hands, whispering, "Don't cry, Thank-You, don't cry." I don't even know why I wanted to cry so badly. I felt like every scared feeling I ever felt in my life was all rolled up into one big ball, and it chose to sit right in the middle of my throat, choking me up. This time should be no different than all them other times I been rejected, but it is. It is different because I'm a different bean than who I was then, and Miss Clara different from all them other fake mamas I done stayed with.

I held my breath, each step they took closer to the room, was one less breath that entered my body. In the back of my mind I know that Miss Clara love me, but when you ain't never experienced a real-life mama, you ain't got nothing to compare it to. I know she love me, but that don't gotta mean she want me to be her very own real-life baby girl. She still so young and pretty. I know that she could find herself a husband, and have her own real-life babies. "Thank-You, baby," Miss Felix say as they enter the room. "Me and Miss Clara done had a little talk, and there is something we need to talk with you about."

Well, that's all Miss Felix had to say to set me off. I started to cry. I cried so loud and so hard you would think somebody done shot the daddy I ain't never met. I could see them both staring at me, at first shocked, then confused, like they ain't see it coming, and they ain't know what to do. I cried for every little girl that ain't got no mamas and daddies, and they tired. They souls tired from being rejected all the time. "Baby girl, why you crying?" Miss Clara say as she walk over to the couch where I was sitting. She took the seat next to me, and patted her thighs so I knew where I could put my head.

Miss Clara rubbed my back, gently stroked my forehead with fingers so gentle, like they was made for crying babies. She rubbed my back till I felt my eyes getting heavy, like a pair of pants hanging out to dry in the rain. Before I fell asleep, Miss Clara's voice entered my ears as a whisper. "Felix, you could go on and see yourself out tonight, I'm gonna stay right here with Thank-You till she fall asleep, and when she wake up I'll let her know that I wanna be her mama. If you have time to stop by tomorrow, we can get the adoption paperwork started."

I was so excited all I wanted to do was jump up and kiss them both. I didn't get the chance to hear Miss Felix respond, by the time she went to speak my eyes was already closed, and I was sleeping like a baby. Thirteen years of exhaustion settled into my little body like it ain't never settled in before, and for the first time in my life I fell asleep knowing what it was like to have a real-life mama.

16.

Josephine

One would imagine being cooped up in a room for months would drive anyone insane. That seems like the least of my worries these days. I welcome insanity. I welcome anything that would release my mind from the prison that it has been placed in. My only contact with the outside world has been letting the maids come in to clean up my room, drop off food that I barely eat, and do the laundry that I never wear. Mother doesn't bother coming in here. The most she does is stand outside and scream like a drunken maniac, which has subsided a bit over the past few days. I'm not sure what she's telling the folks in her bridge club or her charities, but she isn't nagging me anymore, so I assume she thought of a plausible story and ran with it.

I'm happiest in my room. I don't do much anymore but lay on my bed anyway. I don't feel like I'm missing out on anything fantastic. I have my window if I want to spy on the world, my books if I want to read about the world, and my diary if I want to write about the world. No one is missing me either. I don't have any friends, Mother and Father don't care as long as their friends aren't asking questions, and the help has always been too scared to talk to me in case they get hollered at. It seems these days the only person I talk to is God, and that consists of a lot of yelling on my part.

I have been writing more and more in my journal. The past few days it seems like my thoughts are spilling out like paint on a canvas, covering its pages with more life than I have lived. I've been writing any and everything: stories, thoughts, dreams, ideas, and poems. My latest poem came to me in my sleep. I dreamt I was floating over my body, watching myself as I laid on my bed, words flowing through the recorder that rests in my mind, locking themselves into a vault, waiting to be written down later.

> Brown girl don't cry.
> I see you laying with tears in your eyes;
> eyelashes hiding lies,
> lies that rip through your soul
> like a lion into a gazelle.
> Brown girl don't cry.
> The shadow stands over you
> watching you lay,
> hiding the smile on its face
> with a mask of pain.
> Brown girl don't cry.
> Suck it in,
> close your eyes,
> let your pain hide.
> Brown girl don't cry.

Rest your head on your pillow
feel your soul die.
Brown girl don't cry.

I get as many as these thoughts down in my diary as I can. Hoping to leave them as a relic in the wake of my existence, to be found written on the walls of my bedroom like some prehistoric cave dweller leaving remnants of their past. It is the only outlet that I have, the only way that I can cope with the thought of what has happened to me. I told no one. How would anyone understand? Mother and Father would never believe that Uncle John would ever hurt me, let alone do the unthinkable. Sometimes I don't even believe it. I wonder if I'm imagining it in my mind. If perhaps I fell asleep that night in the book shop and was never awakened by a shadow, but somewhere in my perverted mind I made all of it up.

My mind spins in circles. Each thought bringing with it a new pain to my belly, a clenching, a tightness. This is what disgust feels like. I don't know if I am disgusted with Uncle John or with myself. Why would I fall asleep like that? Why would I allow him to call me beautiful all of the time? I made this happen to me. I sent him the wrong message. I was so lonely, maybe he felt like that was what he needed to do to show me love. Maybe I wanted it to happen. All of these thoughts end up in my diary. Nothing gets spared, and nothing gets left out.

I've thought so many times about that night; the cycle is endless and exhausting. After Uncle John lifted himself off of me, I couldn't look at him in his face. I should have stared him directly in his eyes. When he brought me home, he kept his hand on my knee in the truck the whole way here. I should have screamed. I should have run. Instead, I did nothing. When I got home Mother and Father had already received a telephone call from him saying that we'd been working late in the shop reorganizing the bookshelves. I lied with my silence. I lied by not speaking the truth when I walked in the front door. I should have told somebody.

The more I think, the more the core of my soul tightens its grip on my stomach, sending a wrenching pain throughout my entire body. I lay, my body curled up into a little ball, arms wrapped around my belly, praying that whatever little food I have sitting in there stays right where it's supposed to. The prayer was made obsolete by the pain, without my being able to stop it, or get up in time to save my covers or nightgown, my body shed its heaviness, spilling puddles of my own vomit onto my bed.

17.

Thank-You

"Thank-You Pruitt." Hmmm, that name sound so pretty when I say it out loud. I ain't never had no last name before. It always just been "Thank-You." Some people say "Thank" was my first name and "You" was my last name, but that ain't never felt right. "Thank-You Pruitt." I gotta learn how to write that. Now that Miss Clara gonna be my mama, she say she gotta get me caught up with my reading and writing, so I could start going to school. Right now she just teaching me at home, so I don't feel no kind of way round them other kids.

It feel real nice having a mama. Miss Clara tell me that's what I could call her now, "Mama." That's my teeth new favorite word. Sometimes it's hard for me to keep them in my mouth when I say it. It don't even matter what I'm saying it for, as soon as that "ma" leave my lips that smile start forming, the one that make the corners of my mouth touch my ears. "Excuse me, Mama." I smile. "Mama, I gotta use the bathroom." I smile again. I heard somebody say once, "It's the little things in life that count." Like me, being able to say, "Mama."

"The little things." That sound real nice, except saying, "Mama" ain't no little thing to me. Like smelling flowers ain't no little thing either. Whoever said that must not have ever realized the effort it take for a flower to grow? It just don't happen outta nothing. Everything positive and beautiful should be the biggest things in life, the things we talk 'bout, the things we put our effort into thinking 'bout all the time. I hear grown folks in the library, on the street, even in church talking 'bout all the bad stuff goin' on in they lives and in other peoples' lives. They don't leave no energy to talk 'bout the good things. They make all that bad stuff so big, they got big ole gray clouds hanging over they heads all the time. Me, I ain't got me no gray cloud. I got sunshine, and flowers, and squirrels. That's what I got hanging over my head, cuz my big things is everything that make me smile.

The only thing that cross my mind sometimes is when I think how my real-life mama feel. The one whose blood running through my veins, filling my heart with the things it need to keep it beating. I wonder if she sad, thinking I trying to replace her. Or if she happy, cuz I finally know what it feel like to have a mama hold me and cuddle me when I having bad dreams. I think she happy, cuz my mama an angel, and angels gotta be happy singing and dancing up in Heaven, like they just souls living on top of the world. Miss Felix say that angels is the ones that guide us, and protect us. She say that my mama guiding me and protecting me every day. So I know she brought me here.

"Baby girl, is you ready?" I hear my new mama say. I'm going to the library by myself today to pick out a new book to practice my reading with. In summer we was able to go every day together.

Mama was teaching her craft classes, and I hung out with Mister Clarence before my reading lessons. But, now fall is here, and she real busy. She planning a big fundraising event for the community. She ain't really get into telling me details, but I know it must be important cuz Mama ain't have me walk to the library by myself yet, and today I ain't got no choice.

'C'mon now, baby girl, I packed you a sandwich and some of that banana pudding that you love. I'm gonna walk you down to the sidewalk. You sure you remember how to get there? You know you ain't supposed to get in nobody car, and if somebody try grabbing you, you scream as loud as you ever heard a scream in yo life. And you let them little legs bring you home as fast as a rock-et, you hear?" I nod politely. "Yes, Mama. I know exactly where I'm going, and if anybody try grabbing on me I'm gonna run fast as lightning."

Mama and me walk out to the sidewalk holding hands. She looking so beautiful today, as she do every day. The sunlight shining off of her deeply bronzed skin got her looking like one of my favorite kind of pennies. She holding on to my hand so tight, it almost feel like she don't want to let it go. "Mama, you gonna have to let my hand go so I can start walking now, okay. Don't worry I gonna be just fine." She look down at me like she was using every force behind them soulful brown eyes not to cry. "You go on now, baby, just be brave and strong like you are. Mister Clarence gonna call me when you reach the library so I know you're safe. Make sure you stop by his desk first, and I'll be there to pick you up soon as I'm done here." With the final, "Yes, Ma'am," leaving my lips, I was on my way.

There is something so liberating 'bout being able to take a walk by yourself. That's another one of them big things I appreciate. It's a symbol of coming into an age where you are trusted to do something alone, even if it's just a walk. I know Mama was scared though; I could still feel the pressure of my hand in hers as she gave it one last squeeze before she let it go. I know she ain't scared that I'm not gonna do what I'm supposed to do, she scared cuz this world got some folks living in it that do some real bad things.

But today ain't a day to think 'bout them people. Today is a day full with sunshine, beautiful flowers, and smiling faces of the neighbors as I pass by them, waving politely. The houses get larger and larger as I make my way toward the library. When I'm walking with Mama, we so busy talking 'bout life, her imparting wisdom on me, that I ain't never really see all that there is to see round here. I'm excited to be able to fully take it all in, embracing the reality of my present truth. Mama call it "the power of the present." She say that's when you able to pay attention and focus on everything that happening to you in the moment that it's happening to you in.

Right now I'm enjoying practicing my reading, trying to sound out all the street names. Some of them too hard to read, but others are fun to sound out, "'Ja-ack-ssson Ss-street.' 'Fill-moo-re Laaa-ne.' 'Juu-nni-per Tr-aaa-ce.'" I stopped dead in my tracks as I began to make sense of the last street sign that I read, my hands suddenly wet, overflowing with beads of sweat. "'Ju-ni-per Tr-ace,'" I say again. The blood in my body, the same blood that I got from my real-life mama, left my face, shooting through my veins to accelerate the beating of my heart.

18.

Josephine

"The maid found her laying in a pool of her own vomit and blood. The help tried to contact her parents, but they were unable to get a hold of anyone. They had the gardener bring her in two days ago." I could hear the hum of voices around me, the faint noise of machines buzzing and beeping next to my ears. I tried opening my eyes, but they just felt so heavy. "Josephine, Josephine Dieu, if you can hear me blink your eyes." I must have done a good job, because I heard her say "Good girl. That's real good."

As I start coming to, the noises become clearer, more distinct. The owners of the voices are unknown to me. Have I lost my memory? I'm unable to recognize much. "Josephine, I need you to follow the sound of my voice, try to open your eyes now." Trying to follow the sound of a voice when you are coming out of a deep sleep is like trying to find the surface of the water when you have been trapped under for a long time. You can see the glimmer of light the sun creates as it cracks through the surface, beckoning you to follow its path. It's like the sun is speaking, "Josephine, open your eyes. I am showing you the way, follow my voice, baby girl."

"I am looking for you, sun. Where are you?" I say back with my thoughts. "I am trying to find my way out of this darkness, help me." My eyes begin to bring in the light from the sun, radiating through my soul, feeling as if my spirit were rising out of my body into an ethereal flame, rising, rising, my heart racing, I'm rising.

Suddenly, all goes still in my mind. My eyes open, the haziness of the room begins to come into focus. I can see the face of an angel, skin white like that of a dove, her voice sweet and melodic. "Josephine, good morning, sweetheart." I find the strength, not sure from where, to say back to my angel, "Am, am I in Heaven?" With a slight smile, the angel replied, "No, baby, but you are in the hospital. My name is Nurse McCall, and I've been waiting to see those pretty eyes."

"Hospital?" I respond. My voice so tiny, I can barely hear it myself. "Yes, you've been here for almost two days now, sleeping like a princess." I must have been real tired I thought to myself. I can't believe I slept for so long without anybody being able to wake me up. I don't even know when I fell asleep, or how I got here. The last thing I can recall is feeling my belly hurting so badly, like my sadness was beginning to take over my entire body. "Where are Mother and Father?" I squeeze out of my throat. Not sure what response I expected back. But I wasn't surprised when the nurse said that she wasn't sure. "I've been hoping you'd be able to tell us how to contact them."

The tears warmed my skin, as they passed by my tiny cluster of freckles. I looked at the nurse, unsure of how to respond. I knew that Mother and Father had been made aware. I knew that they just didn't see fit to make time out of their busy schedule to come see why their baby girl was in the hospital. The nurse, noticing my tears, must have thought it best to not ask me any more questions, and got up to walk out of the room. "Nurse, before you go, do you know how I got here, or why?" She stared at me for a moment, calibrating the wisdom in my eyes before responding, "I believe your gardener brought you in, love, and we are doing all we can to figure out why you are so sick. When we do, and we get your parents in here, we'll all have a talk." With that, she was gone, turning the lights off on her way out.

What do I do now? My body felt exhausted despite having been asleep for a couple of days. My thoughts creating a whirlwind of confusion and emotions, causing the shallow pounding that was once subtle in my head to bring itself into a state of full awareness. Making my body aware of its presence with its massive thump, thump, thump. I closed my eyes, and prayed for God to release the pain. Just then, I heard what I assume to be the footsteps of Nurse McCall. I felt her warm hands as they gently touched my arm, injecting whatever magic potion into my blood to stop the pounding in my head and send me straight into a light sleep. As my eyes close again, I whisper, "Thank you," not to the nurse who whispered back, "You're welcome," but to God, for finally doing something that I asked.

19.

Thank-You

$\mathcal{I}$ ain't got no business going down no Juniper Trace. "I don't even know which house I would be going to," I mutter quietly to myself as I continue my walk to the library. The early afternoon sun hitting my face, causing my freckles to dance as small beads of sweat flow freely past them. I don't even know why I wanna go there anyway, I don't even know them people. "The Dieu family," I say to myself, the sound of the words rolling off my tongue feels so familiar in a way that just ain't making no sense. I didn't even ask my new mama what she knew 'bout them. She probably gonna think I'm either crazy or real nosy. Neither of which I want her thinking before she officially adopt me.

I just need to do what I was told and keep making my way over to the library. With every step I take, I doubt my decision. I know going straight to the library is what I'm supposed to do, and I'm a real good listener. I don't like to get in no trouble with nobody. I especially don't want my new mama thinking I can't be trusted to walk alone. But if I don't at least walk down Juniper Trace, my mind ain't gonna ease up none. It won't take me but a few extra minutes if I walk real fast and don't stop to smell no flowers.

With my mind made up, I walk as quickly as I can back the way I came. I passed Juniper Trace only a few moments before, so I knew I wasn't too far off. As I approached the street sign, I stopped to look up at it. I sounded it out one more time just to make sure I was going down the right street, "'Ju-nni-per Tr-ace.'" Yup, that sound like the one, I confirm to myself as I quickly make my way in the direction my heart was telling me to go. I didn't even know what I was looking for as my little feet carried me on my journey, giving each and every house a good stare down as I passed by. The more I walked the lonelier the street became, and quite frankly, the scarier. The houses got bigger, the front lawns I had become accustomed to, lined with beautiful flowers and wrap around porches, were now being surrounded by giant guard gates. Some with golden lions perched high on top stone pillars.

"Turn around, Thank-You," I say to myself half in my mind, half out loud. Feeling betrayed by my better judgment for leading me down this street. What was I thinking? There were no friendly neighbors for me to wave to, no familiar faces or voices coming from behind pretty florally clad curtains. This street was lined with mansions that looked more like prisons than anything else. The most life coming from inside their walls was the sound of seemingly large dogs barking madly at the strange little girl entering into their world.

I set my mind to walk to the end of the street, and if finding nothing then I would turn around, never to think of it again. As I reach close to the end, I see one last house. It's clearly larger than all of the others, except this one had no iron fence, no lions perched high atop pillars keeping watch, just a long pathway leading up to what looked like two giant wooden doors. There was barely any movement coming from the house, just a few leaves blowing in the wind. It was the middle of the day and it still exuded a sense of darkness. This house, made me feel sad. I had to muster up all of my courage to keep my feet moving in its direction, I just needed to get far enough to see the name on the mailbox.

As I approached the walkway, I realized that the mailbox wasn't standing outside like most homes around here. Matter of fact, I didn't know where it would be. I think I seen once or twice that some homes got mailboxes over by their front doors. I can't imagine why on earth this big ole house ain't got a stand up mailbox. Nervously, I made myself venture closer, figuring if I made it this far I may as well go all the way. Praying that I wasn't figuring wrong.

My feet feel like they dragging lead all the way up the path to the giant doors. I tell myself to just keep on moving. "C'mon feets." The closer I get, the heavier they get, the darker the house seem to get. My breath speed up, coming in and out of my body faster than I'm thinking about running away. Finally, I reach the front of the porch. This house so big the front porch looking like it could fit five or six of my mama porches in them. It's big, but it's empty. It ain't got no rocking chairs, no swing, no hammock, nothing to serve tea on. It just looking lonely. The porch so big I still got me like twenty more steps to take before I get up to seeing the name on the mailbox, which was hung prim and proper next to the doorbell. I gingerly made my way, taking care not to step on too many creaking wooden floorboards. I get up to that mailbox, and see it. The name I knew I was gonna find. "THE DIEU RESIDENCE." I exhaled, and just when that last sigh of relief was coming out of my body, the front door opened.

20.

Josephine

"Wake up, child," I hear my mother's stern voice piercing the veil of sleep that's covering my eyes. "Mother, you're here," I manage to whisper with sleep still lingering on my breath and in my eyes. I must have slept for a few more hours, because I can no longer see the stream of light sneaking in through the slim open spaces of the dense hospital curtains. "Who else would be here, child? You ask the stupidest questions," Mother snapped back. "What kind of trouble did you get yourself into? I have fundraisers to plan, bridge club to organize, and you want to be selfish and cause all of this nonsense."

"Mother, I'm so happy you're here, I didn't get myself into any trouble. I don't even know what happened. One minute my belly was hurting real bad, and the next I was waking up here." I wasn't sure what to feel or think talking to Mother. I know my parents aren't the best, but I was kind of excited to get a bit of sympathy from them. That dream was short lived and shattered by her temper, accompanied by the smell of brandy hanging off of her breath like a Christmas tree ornament. All she did was stare at me in contempt, wishing she were somewhere else, anywhere else.

"Is Father here too?" I whisper, not looking up at her face. "Do you really think your father has time for your foolishness? I hope being in that hospital bed is helping you to realize that your life could be much worse. You could be homeless, filthy and poor, sleeping in these beds for shelter. Instead, you're a good-for-nothing ingrate who makes herself sick by staying locked up in that room of yours, not eating, expecting people to take pity on your miserable self, while the rest of us work hard making money to take care of you." Mother's brown face was red with frustration, drunkenness, and annoyance.

"Are you okay, Mrs. Dieu?" the doctor's voice coming as a surprise to us both, as he walked casually into the room. "Oh yes, doctor, I am fine. I'm just so worried about my precious baby, I must have gotten carried away with emotion." The grin that spread itself across her face looked like something she borrowed from Satan himself. Mother is good at this game; she has been playing it for so long. She is so used to being unhappy, it's like a switch that she can turn on and off. I almost feel sorry for the unsuspecting victim that will never know what she is truly capable of. I say "almost sorry" because in some way, I think they are lucky. In fact, I wish I were them: a stranger who gets to receive her smile, over the daughter that gets to feel her terror.

"Is Mr. Dieu going to join us, ma'am?" The doctor spoke, unaware of my mother's true self. "Oh no, doctor. Mr. Dieu is always so busy working. Running the family trust is a hard day's work you know. I don't ever see him myself. It's a lonely life I live. I bet a handsome man like you would never know what it feels like to be lonely?" Mother was talking in a way I have never heard her speak before, looking like a turkey, ready to gobble up whatever words fall out of the doctor's mouth. She was making all kinds of weird faces at him, eyes a little bit closed, opening real wide whenever he went to speak, lips puffed out like a largemouth bass. I don't think she realizes how absolutely silly she looks.

The doctor himself looks like he's two minutes past uncomfortable, his feet are pointed toward the door like he's ready to run out of the room. "Well, there are some things that I would like to discuss with you and Mr. Dieu as soon as possible. Do you think he can meet us sometime tonight, ma'am?" As soon as the last word left the doctor's mouth, I watched mother's face switch from concerned parent to praying mantis, revealing her true self to the doctor. "What does my family look like to you people? Clearly we are too busy for this nonsense. What is it that you are not understanding? Do you need to go back to college to comprehend what I'm telling you? My family makes it possible for your measly, little paycheck to be possible. Do you understand that?" The doctor put his head down, not saying anything else to Mother. He politely excused himself, letting the door shut behind him.

I couldn't believe it was so easy for Mother to get rid of the doctor. I think we were both a bit stunned when he walked out. Unfortunately for me, his exit didn't deter her rampage, nor did it cause her to stop ranting and raving about how big of an idiot she thought he was. She couldn't believe that he didn't even tell her how long they would be keeping me, or what was wrong with me. Just as Mother was in the middle of saying something else mean and nasty about the hospital staff, the door to the room opened. This time it wasn't the doctor. It was another lady, much younger than the doctor. She wasn't wearing a nurse's uniform. She was dressed in a business suit, clearly too large for her small body. She couldn't have been any older than twenty-one, and smiling like she was fresh out of college.

"Good evening, my name Ms. Clark. I'm the social worker here for the hospital. The doctor wanted me to come in to talk to y'all 'bout what goin' on." Mother looked like she was getting ready to chew this girl up alive, another unsuspecting victim. "Who do you think you are, coming in here speaking to us like you have no education or home training? Do you know who I am?" The nice girl looked at Mother, continuing to smile, replying only, "No, ma'am. I do not know who you is, nor do I give a rats behind. I am here for the sole purpose of this baby, and this baby only."

Mother was still going off on her wild yelling spree. "What the hell makes you think my baby is any of your low-class business?" Ms. Clark, still keeping her composure, looked my mother square in her face, expression unchanging, showing signs of experience far beyond her years. "First of all, Mrs. Dieu, I don't care how wealthy you is, you ain't above the law, and you ain't above treating your daughter right. But, for argument's sake, let's say it is too late for me to save this poor child from a mother like you. But it ain't too late for me to save the baby growing inside her belly."

The last sound I heard was that of mother's body smacking against the cold, hard hospital floor, before my own eyes rolled as far back into my head as eyes could roll.

21.

Thank-You

When fear hits you, it take all the courage and strength you got in your bones to not faint. You could feel the blood rushing out yo head, causing a sensation like spinning in a million circles on the Merry-Go-Round. That fear can overtake your body if you let it, causing all kinds of things to happen. When that front door opened, I ain't never been so scared in my life. It felt like my body was ready to drop and hit the floor. Can you imagine my new mama getting a call that her new baby done dropped dead of fear, doing something she know she wasn't supposed to be doing in the first place?

If it wasn't for the love I got for Mama, maybe I would have fainted. But, I don't have time for all that today. I still gotta get myself to the library so Mister Clarence can call her to let her know I got there safely. I had to be brave. The figure that stood in the doorway was that of an older woman, not quite elderly, wearing skin the color of cinnamon sticks, yet pale in the oddest way.

She looked worn down and ragged, like she ain't never been showed by nobody how to smile. That make me feel sorry for her teeth. She looked like she was beautiful once, a long time ago. Before her eyes grew those bags under them, looking like they carrying all the weight of the world. They so big you can barely count the freckles hiding underneath all that puffiness. Even when she opened the door she ain't smile. "What do you want little girl?" she say. Her voice croaked and eerie like she ain't spoken to nobody in a long time.

Be brave, Thank-You, I think to myself, *just be brave.* "Good afternoon, ma'am. My name Thank-You. I was just passing by to say hello. I learning to read over at the library. Your library, ma'am, and I was real interested to meet you. I ain't even know why? I just figured since I was on my way I'd just stop by." The lady stared, not showing any expression, just a blank stare. "Look, little girl, I don't know who sent you, but I don't have any money or time for you, you understand? Go on and get out of here now, before I set my dogs out on you. They like eating little, stupid children like you." That's all she said before she slammed the door in my face. I guess that's all she had to say, it don't get no meaner than that.

I turned my back to the front door, ready to run as quickly as I could toward the library named after this nasty old lady, wondering if her whole family was nasty like her. I just had one thing on my mind to do before I left. I hopped off of her front porch and walked over to the giant oak tree standing as crooked as she was in her yard. I picked all of the wild flowers I could find growing around its base, apologizing to them as I took them from their families, hoping they weren't hurt in any way. I explained that they were giving their lives for the best cause ever, to bring someone a bit of happiness.

I picked the flowers as gently and as quickly as I could before hurriedly making my way back up to the front porch. I rested the wildflowers by the foot of those giant double doors, stood on my tippy toes to ring the doorbell, then turned and ran as quickly as I could to the library. I ran so fast my breath could barely keep up with my lungs, all the while thinking about that mean lady, wondering what life could've done to her to make her that way.

22.

Josephine

It took three nurses, one social worker, and one security guard to keep my mother from beating my head in. "Calm down, Mrs. Dieu," screamed one. "Get her out of here," screamed another. The voices all jumbled together, causing the buzzing sensation in my head to worsen by the second. I was passed out for a bit longer than a few moments, that's what I'd been told. The social worker, Ms. Clark, must have alerted the hospital staff that she had two cold turkeys on her hands.

They must have gotten Mother up before me, because when the room came into focus again, they had her propped up in a chair, a wet rag on her forehead, and a bag on her lap to catch vomit. One nurse was fanning her, while Ms. Clark was busily writing in the notebook she's been carrying since she walked in here. I wonder what she was writing down. "*Josephine Dieu, unwed thirteen-year-old girl, carrying a baby in her belly. Looking as though she had it coming. Her mother is a psychopath.*" I would imagine it to sound something along those lines.

The thought of the word *"baby"* shot chills up and down my spine. Mother must have had a similar thought in that exact moment, because that's when all the blood and life came rushing back into her face. She jumped so quickly out of the chair she was sitting in, I thought it was going to get up with her. I never heard my mother speak to me like she did that day. She forgot every ounce of higher-education grammar and laid it on me like never before, revealing bits of a secret past life. "You stupid lil' ungrateful whore," she screeched. "That's what you been doin', actin' like you a innocent lil' angel, but you ain't. You just a dumb lil' whore like dem whores yo daddy be runnin' round with. You were supposed to be a boy, I ask God every day why I was cursed with you."

With every nasty word out of her mouth, she took another step closer to me. By the time she finished her sentence Mother was looming over my body. Paralyzed by fear, I did nothing. Like the night with the shadow; I did nothing. I deserve whatever beating I get from Mother. She was telling the truth. I did a bad thing, and this was my consequence. "Get on away from that girl, Mrs. Dieu. You ain't laying not one finger on her, you hear, or I'm gonna have you put in jail so fast, yo money ain't gonna do no more than give you something to wipe yo ass with."

Mother's face was full of hatred, anger, ignorance, embarrassment, and disappointment. A combination not to be taken lightly. She ignored every word that was coming out of Ms. Clark's mouth, inching closer toward my face. That's when the noise started, and people came rushing in. My world stood still, unmoving, everything happening around me was a blur rushing past my face. Mother's screaming turned to tears. The security guard and nurses rushed in to restrain her, eventually carrying her out of the room, exhausted.

"You gonna be okay, baby girl. We'll let yo mama calm down, and when she does I'll go out there and talk to her again. For now, I need you to help me understand what going on, okay?" Ms. Clark was really sweet. She looked at me with a kindness in her eyes that I had not yet received from another soul. "Yes, ma'am, Mother just gets carried away sometimes. I don't know how I can help you understand what's going on though. I really don't even know myself." Reading the puzzled expression on my face, she knew that I wasn't lying. I don't understand how a baby got into my belly. I figured it was because of what the shadow did that night in the bookshop. I knew it was something terrible, but before that night I knew nothing of what boys looked like under their pants, or what they did with it, or that they had babies in there waiting to be put inside of little girls.

Ms. Clark took a seat in the chair next to my bed, she placed the notebook down that she'd been carrying around, and took my hand in hers. Her hands were so soft and gentle, despite them being as thin as sticks. They had a warmth about them that was so comforting I wished for a moment that I were her baby. "Baby girl, do you know how you got this baby growing inside you?" Her eyes were welcoming, beckoning the words to fall from my lips. But how was I supposed to tell her what I had done? Everybody would know, and Uncle John's wife would never forgive me. "No, ma'am," I say staring down at my hands as they rested nervously in hers.

"Okay now, sugar. I won't pressure you into talking, that ain't what I'm here for. I'm here to be your friend. But when you're ready to tell me what happened, or who did this to you, I promise to listen without judging you, okay. I know this all real scary. I want you to be able to trust me so we can figure this whole mess out, together." Ms. Clark's eyes were telling the truth, I could feel it. I could feel that she probably didn't have an easy life with everything handed to her like me, and yet here she was, sitting next to my bed, holding my hand, grateful that she wasn't me. I looked at her with those honest eyes she wore with pride, and did what I thought was best. I kept on lying.

"I don't know how this baby got in my belly, ma'am. Somehow it just ended up in there. Maybe I sat on the toilet seat by accident once and the baby crawled inside of me?" I tried to continue looking her in the eyes as I lied, but I couldn't. I kept looking away, hoping she would decide that my story was believable enough. I know there is more than one way for ladies to get babies in their bellies, that's what my Sunday school teacher said Christmas was all about. I clearly remember her saying that baby Jesus came straight from Heaven and landed right in his mother's belly. Maybe something like that could have happened to me too?

Ms. Clark didn't push the conversation like I prayed she wouldn't. God sure is listening to me more and more these days. But she did let me know that I would be staying in the hospital for a while longer, because they aren't used to having girls my age with babies inside of them. She said they have to monitor me to make sure that my little body can handle what's going to happen to it, and when I'm stable enough they'll send me home with Mother. She'll also be checking in with me as often as she can.

When she got up to excuse herself she gave my hand a tight squeeze, and made a face clearly showing what I thought to be pity, a bit of sadness, mingled with kindness and love. "Alright now, baby girl, get some rest. We don't want you having no more fainting spells, we gotta keep you both healthy. I'll be in to sit with you again real soon." With that she slid quietly out of the room, leaving my mind whirling with confusion, exhaustion, and fear.

PART THREE

Winter

23.

Thank-You

Backwards, forwards, backwards, forwards, backwards, forwards, I rock. I'm beginning to understand why it is Mama be rocking in this chair so much. Each motion of this is done with purpose. I decide if I want the chair to go backwards, then I decide if I want it to go forwards. The chair help, cuz if I don't stop it, then it will keep going a few more times on its own, but that's a decision too: whether or not I stop the rocking. Mama say that everything we do in life is a choice. She say that in order for us to grow as human beans we gotta practice being mindful of every choice we make. "Mindful," I whisper to myself, muffled by the slow and steady creak of the rocking. I've been learning more and more 'bout what it means to be mindful every day with Mama. I been keeping my mind full of things that gonna help me make wise decisions. Well, I been trying at least, cuz there is one thing that got me feeling like I ain't doing too good of a job. That's why I been rocking in this chair so much.

I got something sitting heavy in my soul. So heavy in fact, going to church ain't even holding no joy for me cuz I know that God know what I been up to. Thing is, I can't quite figure out if it's right, or if it's wrong. I've asked but ain't received no answer yet. Every motion I make in this rocking chair is a reminder of the choices I been making. "Baby girl, you gonna catch cold out there sitting and swaying on that chair for so long. Why don't you come on inside, and I'll make you some hot cocoa?" I take a deep breath, the cold air whipping through my lungs, causing a slight sting. "Yes, Mama, cocoa sound real yummy." That wasn't a lie, cocoa does sound real yummy. I just ain't excited for it like the tone of my voice let on.

I hop off the rocking chair, my feet landing firmly on the cold wooden floorboards of the porch. The sun is now beginning to go down, and I'm feeling more and more like I need to spill the contents of my heart out to Mama. I'm just so scared. I ain't even adopted yet, and already I got me a big ole secret. One that I've been keeping for weeks, months even. What is she gonna think? What is she gonna do? Mama never been vex with me before, but what if this secret so big, she not only gonna get vex, but she gonna take me back to the home with all them other boys and girls that ain't got no mamas and daddies. All these thoughts running through my head, making me feel sick to my belly. The idea of cocoa hitting my taste buds seem more and more like a real bad idea. "Mama," I call out, hoping to get a sense of where she is. "Baby girl, I'm here in the kitchen. Go on and wash yo hands now, sugar, I got a special treat for you."

The kinder she is, the worse I feel. Obediently, I follow her instructions and head on over to the bathroom. I allow the water to wash over my hands, wishing that it was washing over the stain that spreading itself across my soul. I finish up, dry my hands and walk into the kitchen where Mama is sitting at the table, waiting with two slices of her freshly made "famous" pecan pie and two mugs of steaming hot cocoa. "Come on, baby girl, you best not let all this deliciousness get cold. How do you feel 'bout pecan pie before dinner?" Oh boy, I think. For all the times me and Mama done ate dinner together she ain't never let me eat no dessert before all my food done, and now she letting me eat pie before a bite of dinner even touch my mouth. "Really, Mama? We get dessert before dinner? Thank you, ma'am," I say with an uneasy smile on my face. The contents of my mind so thick, it may as well pull up a seat at the table.

With that, Mama put my little hand in hers, the warmth from her mug of hot cocoa still resting softly on her skin, lending itself to warm my own. Her eyes gaze at me with a sense of concern carefully examining my expressions. She ain't even have to say a word to make her wisdom known.

The thing 'bout Mamas, whether they pushed you out they bellies themselves or not, they know everything. I ain't never really had no experience with a real-life mama before, so I thought only Miss Felix knew the mysteries of the world, its wonders, its secrets, and naturally my secrets. But, the more I get used to my new mama, and she get used to me, the closer I get to realizing that all mamas got this gift, and one day when I'm a mama I hope I get it too.

"Baby girl, something done been on yo mind for a long time now. For weeks and weeks you been sitting at this table with an air of sadness floating all round yo head. I'm getting worried 'bout you, baby. The Thank-You that I know always got sunshine flowing from her beautiful blue eyes. If you got something on yo mind my sweet girl, I'm here to listen."

I let Mama talk, listening intently as she spoke her sweet words to me, my hand still in hers, feeling the love flow between them. I knew it was time to speak the truth. With slight hesitation in my voice, I began. "Mama, since I been going to the library in the fall, every time you let me walk by myself, I don't never go straight there like I say, ma'am." The tears spill from my eyes, as my confession spills from my mouth. "Mama, I been going down Juniper Trace to the house of the lady that own the library. I been going there and leaving flowers by her door. Sometimes I even draw her pictures and leave them too. I know I'm supposed to tell you everything, and that it's dangerous to not tell you where I be going. I was so scared that you was gonna send me away, and every time I go I get more and more scared cuz I ain't tell you from that first moment."

I stopped speaking, watching Mama's eyes gaze at me, not knowing what she was going to say was probably the scariest moment of my existence, even scarier than the first time I met Mrs. Dieu. She cleared her throat, as tears began to flow carefully from her eyes. She squeezed my hand in hers. "I know where you been going all along, my sweet girl. At first I was disappointed in you for not telling me the truth, but I understand why you would be afraid considering the experiences you done had in yo short lifetime." I interjected softly, "So why is you crying, Mama?"

She let out a sigh. "I'm crying because it makes my heart sad to think that you would really believe that I would send you away, and because I don't want you to lump me in the category with all them other fake mamas and daddies. I love you for you, in all yo beautiful forms. Through all them good days we blessed to get, and through days like this where we got to have sad, tough conversations. That's what it means to be a family, Thank-You. We don't need no paperwork from no judge telling us how to love each other. With or without those final adoption papers I am yo mama, and you are my daughter. That is how I love you." I look up at my mama, piece of pie already sitting on my tongue, "I love you too, Mama. I promise I ain't never gonna keep no secrets from you again."

With a smile on both of our faces we eat pie, drink cocoa, and I fill her in 'bout my adventures to bring happiness to mean ole Mrs. Dieu. I still haven't quite figured what it is that has me so drawn to her. Every time I get close to that big, ole, scary-looking house I get a sensation in my heart, one of excitement and joy. Although she never answers when I ring the bell, the excitement is still there because everything I leave for her disappears behind those dark, heavy doors.

24.

Josephine

When someone dies it takes all of the strength you can muster inside of your body to cope with the reality that we are in control of nothing. We ask ourselves questions like, "What is destiny?" We are forced to look God directly in the face and admit defeat. Death does that, brings us to our knees, white flag steadily being raised as we acknowledge that we are the weaker of the spiritual beings. That is what Mother is doing, raising her white flag, surrendering to the life that she was fated. Except, no one has died. Father has simply left.

Although, one would never assume there is no funeral being held in the Dieu household, being that Mother has taken to wandering around the house wearing all black, showing signs of despair anytime someone merely looks in her direction. Using her weekly bridge club gathering as an audience to her latest theatrical display to be titled "deserted wife, and mother."

It was really only a matter of time before Father left us. He finally managed to plant the seed of a son into willing soil. I learned that from Ms. Clark. She says that human beings are better off being called "human beans," because that's what we are. She says that humanity is constantly evolving and growing like plants, and when a woman becomes pregnant it is because a man has planted a seed inside of her womb, just like planting a seed inside of the earth. And it is the job of a mother to nourish, water, and feed the seed until it grows and blossoms into a beautiful flower. Father is somewhere out in the world with his new family, and I am here with Mother, silently grateful that he is gone, as I'm sure Mother is also.

It is a strange dynamic, a week ago I was laying in my hospital bed wondering what Father would say to me when we finally saw each other. I was in the hospital for two months, and not once did he come to visit, nor did he ever send a "hello" with Mother. None of that matters now. He is gone, and mother is dawning an all-black wardrobe, hosting bridge club with a constant stream of counterfeit tears in her eyes, and I am back at home trying to assimilate myself to a sense of normalcy; a word that has long lost its meaning in my life. Over the course of the last few days I have found myself missing my hospital bed. This house holds so much sadness. Father's leaving representing the only joyous occasion. I am concerned for the child growing within me. How am I to nourish the seed in my belly when I, myself, am planted in a bed of rocks?

Ms. Clark is expected for her first home visit this afternoon. She has been a great comfort to me over these past two months, and I think she may even be my friend. I've never really had one of those before, so I'm not quite sure if I could call her that, but she's as close as I've ever come to experiencing friendship. She is much younger than one would expect a social worker to be. She is twenty-two years old, she's not married, and she doesn't have any babies of her own. She is really pretty in an average kind of way, beautiful deep brown skin and eyes, and she always has her notebook and pen handy to write down whatever catches her attention. I think that's why she is so smart, she pays attention to everything, even the things that aren't spoken out loud.

I always look forward to the time we spend together. It wasn't always like that though. The first few weeks in the hospital were rough. Mother was constantly screaming at somebody, anybody who would allow it, and Ms. Clark was constantly trying to figure out how it is I came to get this seed in my belly. I never actually told her what happened, still can't get myself to speak the words out loud. Eventually she stopped asking me questions. I can only hope that she gave up, but something tells me that she is just waiting patiently for the words to come bursting out of my mouth. Maybe they will one day, but definitely not today. I've finally gotten to a place with Mother where we can tolerate being in the same room at the same time without her trying to strangle me. I'm sure a lot of that is due to her attention being turned toward her failed marriage, as well as Ms. Clark warning her that if is she so much as stresses me out for one moment she will have every news reporter in town anonymously tipped off about the wealthy Dieu family and their closet full of secrets. Needless to say, Mother has been on her best behavior.

"Josephine," my mother carefully calls my name from outside of my bedroom door. "Yes, Mother," I reply. At only four months pregnant, I have full mobility of my body, but I am not allowed to do much walking around as per the doctor's orders. It is strange that Mother is calling my name from outside the door, as she, along with the help have been walking in and out of my room as they please since I have been home. "Josephine, you have a visitor." The tone in her voice high pitched and jolly. A visitor? Oh, Ms. Clark is here! Why didn't Mother just say that? "You may enter," I say happily.

As my bedroom door opened, I fixed myself in the bed, so that I could sit up comfortably to talk to Ms. Clark. I had one of the maids go over everything with a dust rag this morning to make sure all of my things were neat and tidy, to make a good first impression. As I looked up my expression turned from excitement to panic. Standing in the open doorway with mother was Aunt Susannah, Uncle John's wife, with a gift in her hand and a smile on her face.

25.

Thank-You

Miss Felix told me a long time ago that dreams is how we humans connect to the infinite universe. They is God's way of sending us messages and signs when our bodies is calm and resting. I used to have lots of dreams when I was real little. I would dream of my real-life mama wearing a white dress standing under a big beautiful tree, her face always a blur, but her voice would speak my name so soft and sweet. She would say, "Thank-You, my sweet girl, I love you." She would giggle and disappear. I haven't dreamt 'bout my real-life mama in a really long time. Up until the past three nights.

I been having the same dream every night. I don't quite know how to put it into words to describe it to Mama so she fully understand. I don't even understand it myself. It just feel so real. It feel like the dream world is my real life, and the world I been living in is actually the dream. It always start out with me hovering over my body watching myself sleep, then I fly into Mama's room and check in on her. Then the voice comes. It's the voice of my real-life mama. I know its hers cuz it's the same voice that used to call to me in my dreams from a long time ago. She say real soft and sweet, "Thank-You, come here. Come to me, Thank-You. I want to show you something." I never see her face; I only hear her voice, and I follow it. Every night I follow her angelic voice, up and through the ceiling. We fly high into the night's sky, gracefully floating through the clouds, dancing past the stars. My mother's giggle beckoning me to follow her. I do. I follow her voice with reckless abandon. It seem as if nothing else matters as she whisper to me, "Come, baby girl. There are treasures to find, secrets to unlock." We fly together, me and my invisible real-life mama. We fly, we dance, we giggle.

We go all over the small town that I now call home. We go past restaurants, houses, even the library. Every night the dream happens the same. We take the same route, we pass the same buildings. I am always elated that I am following my angel-mama. I feel as if I would follow that voice anywhere it called me to go. I know each night that I am being taken to the same place, and each night I willingly go.

Eventually, our destination approaches. I can't see quite where we are going, yet we begin our descent. We float gently down to the ground, hovering ever so slightly over the warm surface of the earth, as I continue to follow the gentle giggle. We hover over Juniper Trace as the voice whispers, "Close your eyes and look with your heart, my beautiful girl." We stop in front of the house. The house that I have come to know only from the outside. The same giant oak tree standing tall in the yard, wild flowers dancing in the wind as they were the first day some of them gave their life to bring joy to the owner of their soil.

I do not know the point in which my feet touch down on the earth. I can feel blades of grass peeking through the crevices between my toes. "Do not be afraid, my sweet girl, look with your heart." The voice whispers this over and over, each time growing fainter than the time before until my angel is gone, leaving me standing alone in front of the dimly lit house. I begin to walk toward the big heavy wooden doors, seemingly larger than life in each dream. As I approach, I faintly hear the moaning and crying of someone clearly in a lot of pain. Fear begins to creep up my legs, wrapping them in a thick layer of darkness. I remind myself of what the angel said. *Do not to be afraid.* I get all the way up to the door, the crying getting louder, my palms is sweaty, veins rushing blood through my body in a state of panic. Again, I remind myself of the voice. *Close your eyes and look with your heart.* I stand on the tips of my toes, poised, and ready to ring the doorbell, when suddenly a burst of air rushes past my face, engulfing my body as the doors burst wide open, illuminating my entire universe in the brightest light I have ever seen. I am surrounded by nothing else but light. I am the light. That is when I wake up, covered in sweat, the voice of my angel echoing in my ears, filling my heart with memories that ain't my own, and my mind with questions that I ain't yet got the wisdom to answer.

26.

Josephine

"Aunt Susannah, what are you doing here?" Those were the first words to fall heavily out of my mouth; my disappointment and fear sending goose bumps up and down my spine. I was at a loss for an appropriate, more cordial greeting. Far worse, I was at a loss for thoughts. My mind blank, staring at the face of the woman whose husband's seed was growing in my young belly. "What is wrong with you, girl? That is not how we greet guests into our home!" Mother was exasperated, her cinnamon skin turning bright shades of red with embarrassment. She put her hand on Aunt Susannah's shoulder to guide her deeper into my room, closer to where I was sitting up in my bed. "Sorry, Susannah. It must be all the medication that those medical doctors have her on. You know she had a horrible stomach infection? She's showing signs of improvement daily, must be the special touch of a mothers love."

Aunt Susannah approached with a sincere look of concern settling appropriately over her creamy white skin, not paying as much attention to Mother as she would have liked. How could she possibly know? *She mustn't?* I thought, my mind slowly beginning to show signs of life. "Hello, Josephine. We were worried when you stopped showing up at the book shop the way you did." As she spoke, she made her way closer to my bed; my pulse beating a bit harder with each step, each word. "To be honest with you, I was real disappointed with you for just quitting on us like that, since your uncle always looks forward to having you in the summer. Then we heard that you were ill from your father, and well, that explained it all. I just wish that you would have told us. It was really selfish of you to just disappear. Uncle John gets so worried about you. He even calls your name out in his sleep."

Listening to Aunt Susannah speak is like hearing birds sing their beautiful melodies early in the morning. Her voice never seems to raise much higher than a raspy whisper, fitting in nicely with her delicate, pale beauty. Her pink lips moving in unison with her rosy cheek bones, in unison with her light green eyes, causing all who listen to want to pay attention to her words effortlessly. The power in her beauty so overwhelming I, myself, was almost overcome, allowing her words to glide easily into my ears, without my even realizing the extent of my disturbance. But at the mere mention of Uncle John's name my spirit writhed in anger, lifting the enchantment brought on by her captivating charm. I was once again, at a loss for words.

For the first time, I wanted to scream at the two women standing in my room. I wanted them gone. My face flushed with excitement, beads of sweat forming on my forehead, I felt as if the only plausible thing to say next, was the truth. The thought of Uncle John calling out to me in his sleep unsettled every inch of my soul, taking me back to the moment when his sweaty body was on top of my own, pressing me into the uncomfortable hard floor beneath us as he pressed himself against me, inside me. The truth began to form itself angrily on the tip of my tongue, ready to burst from my mouth as I would imagine fireballs from the mouth of a dragon. I wanted to hurt them, like he hurt me. I wanted them for a moment to feel an ounce of the pain that I have been carrying with me for four months. I wanted them for a moment, to know what it felt like to be weak.

I couldn't contain it any longer. It was time. As the words began to pour from my mouth, I was shocked. I was in awe at what was happening, not to me, but through me. I was expecting my mouth to harness the power of my pain, and run wild and free with the truth that it has been aching to speak. But something within me changed. In this moment I became more than just a flower bed for my budding seed, I became a mother. What I was intending to be words of anger, became words of love, and I realized that I did not want my child to live with the knowledge of how they came to be a part of this world. My child would never be labeled "a curse." The desire to protect my unborn baby from feeling the hatred that was building up inside of me was stronger than my desire for anything else. What came out of my mouth instead was a bigger truth than even I knew existed within my soul.

"Aunt Susannah, I truly am sorry for the way that I left things, ma'am. I should have spoken the truth a long time ago, but I was afraid of what others may think of me. There are things in life that as human beans we are destined to experience, and for me, working at your book shop was one of those very things. I was able to fall in love with books, and those books became my best friends, and for that I am grateful. There are reasons that I can't explain as to why I had to leave the way that I did, ma'am, because I fear that the truth should only exist in love, and in God. When the truth is ready, it will blossom as a flower planted in soil, showing the world its magnificent beauty." Aunt Susannah and Mother both stared at me unblinkingly, not quite certain as to what I was speaking about. Neither knowing that battle that was raging on in my mind only moments before.

"Okay then, Josephine. I hope you feel better soon. Oh, and here, before I forget, Uncle John had a present he wanted me to give to his little honey dew." With that, she placed my neatly wrapped gift down on my bedside table and leaned in to give a me hug, which is simple common courtesy where we come from. But that small gesture, although only lasting seconds, sent a ripple through the universe, altering the destiny that would have let hatred win. As Aunt Susannah wrapped her long, sun-kissed arms around me, I was prepared to solely return her hug. But, as her lemonade-colored hair tickled my neck, I whispered silently in her ear. "I love you, and please tell Uncle John, I forgive him."

27.

Thank-You

"Green lizard's blood?" *Where the heck I'm gonna find that?* I think to myself, searching through the contents of Mama's secret potion cabinet. She is finally showing me how to mix potions. I've been waiting on this for a long time, and today is finally the day! "Hmmm." Written on a small vial tucked all the way into the back of the cramped ole cabinet I finally find the gooey green blood I was looking for. I carefully place it between my fingers and hurriedly run back to the kitchen where Mama was waiting with a pot of boiling water. "Good job, baby girl! Now have you decided exactly what kind of potion you want?"

Since I've been telling Mama 'bout my dreams, we been trying to figure them out together. She say that maybe it's my imagination running wild, and my mind so powerful my thoughts 'bout Mrs. Dieu is turning up in my dreams. She say another possibility is maybe my real-life mama is reaching out to me to tell me something. Maybe I'm supposed to help that old lady somehow? We haven't quite figured it out yet, but I asked Mama if she would mix me up a potion to help me, and she said yes. Only thing is, I didn't realize that with making potions you gotta be specific. Mama say that I gotta know exactly the kind of potion I want, so that the magic know what to do when it get in my body.

"Mama, can you make a potion to make her talk to me the next time I leave something out front her door?" My sweet mama lovingly smiled at my question, "No, baby girl. This one has got to be for you and for you alone. It's meant to help you on your journey, and whichever part Mrs. Dieu plays in it you gotta trust destiny to sort all that out." "Yes, ma'am," I reply. I watch as Mama carefully pours the boiling water from the pot into a small glass container no bigger than a tea cup. She watches it intently, making sure she gets the perfect amount. "What about a potion to help me be brave?" I say. Mama thought for a moment, before looking up at me. "Now that's more like it," she said showing a smile so big, I imagined her teeth was dancing.

With an exact potion in mind Mama got to work, mixing and measuring the ingredients that I helped her gather from the pantry and her secret potion cabinet. Using the hot water as the base, she put in three drops of green lizard's blood, shavings of a dried-out weeping willow branch, which to my surprise looked and smelled exactly like cinnamon, and for the third and final ingredient she added a tablespoon of "Heaven's Dust." That one smelled sweet like sugar; it was no surprise that it came from the streets of Heaven. With my potion all mixed and ready to go, Mama poured it into my own special little bottle and handed it over to me with the instructions to put it somewhere safe.

With my potion tucked safely beneath my bedroom pillow, I begin my walk back to the kitchen to help Mama clean up and get ready for dinner. "Ding Dong," the sound of the doorbell sends me on a detour to the front door. "Miss Felix," I say excitedly, as I open the door. My happiness sending signals to the corners of my mouth spreading them as wide as they could possibly stretch. "Oh my goodness, baby girl. You growing so big, and I miss that smile! Come here and give me a hug." I jump up into Miss Felix arms, wrapping my own little arms so tight round her neck, I ain't quite sure if she could breathe or not. My social-worker mama don't come round as often as she used to when I was staying with other fake mamas and daddies. That's cuz she say she trust my new mama with my life, and she know that I being taken real good care of.

I welcome Miss Felix into the house, and tell her that Mama is cleaning in the kitchen. They been friends for so long, I love to see how they get on with each other. Telling jokes and giggling like two girls round my age. Mama tell me that one day I'm gonna have the kind of friendship that she got with Miss Felix. She say when I start going to school in the coming fall it's gonna open me up to a whole new world, one that I ain't never seen before, and I'm gonna be making friends left and right. 'Till then I got Mama, Miss Felix, Mister Clarence at the library, and mean ole Mrs. Dieu, who don't know it, but she my friend too.

I follow behind my social-worker mama as she walk to the kitchen, her thick, brown legs looking the same as they always do in her knee-length skirt, hair pulled back into that familiar bun. "You just in time, Felix. I was just gettin' ready to fix us some dinner," Mama say as we enter into the kitchen. They give each other a big ole hug, the kind that rock from side to side a couple times, letting each other know how glad they is to be back together again.

"What you making for dinner, Clara? You know how I love me some of yo cooking, but you got some funny-looking ingredients sitting out." The look on her face was a mixture of hesitation and unease, both of her thick eyebrows lifted so high, they 'bout getting ready to link up with the rest of the hairs sitting on top her head. Me and Mama chuckle at the same time. She was looking directly at the different components for my "brave" potion. "Oh no, Felix, that ain't dinner. Me and Thank-You was fixing up a special kind of potion. It's plum time I start passing these things down to my baby girl." Mama say, finishing with a smile and a wink. Miss Felix smiled back, a look of intrigue and delight on her face. "I see, this baby girl here is real special. Thank-You, why don't you fill me in on the kind of potions you learning to make?"

I'm not sure if my social-worker mama was asking cuz she really wanted to know, or if she was just being polite and making conversation as we waited for Mama to fix us a yummy dinner, but either way my thoughts began whirling round my head, spinning a mile a minute. Before I knew it I was telling Miss Felix everything that been going on since the last time I saw her. I barely waited for her to take a seat at the kitchen table before I started chattering away. I not only told her 'bout my potion, but I went on to explain to her why it is I wanted to be brave, how I was sneaking off to leave different things in front of a stranger's house without telling my mama, and the dreams I been having 'bout my real-life Mama taking me to the very same house I was sneaking off to for three nights. By the time I was done rambling off to Miss Felix, Mama already had the first piece of chicken battered and ready to be lowered into the pot of sizzling-hot oil.

"Baby girl, you got more things going on in yo life than I got ears to hear 'em all. You been real busy, and this lady must be real special if you been going through all this." She stopped talking for a moment, took a deep breath and continued. "Listen here, little one, when God place something on our heart, even if we don't understand, it's best we follow. Sometimes it ain't even gonna make no sense to us at all. But, eventually all things get revealed in their due time. It's called walking by faith. Baby girl, that mean you gotta close your eyes and see with yo heart." When Miss Felix talk about God and about life, sometime she get this look in her eyes. It's like she go off to another world, like she tapping into some secret source of wisdom hidden deep inside herself.

I love listening to her words when she get that look. I know they coming to me direct from God. Only thing is, I don't quite remember telling her that my real-life mama told me the exact same thing in my dream. "Miss Felix I told you 'bout my real-life mama telling me to close my eyes, and see with my heart?" I asked perplexed. Really, I was talking so fast, I could have said all that to her and just plum forgot? "Clara, that fried chicken smelling so good, I bet you got chickens coming 'round here volunteering to be put into yo pot," Miss Felix joked, catching us all off guard, spreading laughter between us all, causing me to forget my present thoughts, and adversely allowing my question to go unanswered.

28.

Josephine

She didn't blink, nor did she say a word. Her silence acknowledging my truth. Perhaps insight is the ability that one gains when they become a woman, without my noticing, that is what I was becoming. Aunt Susannah and I were now both women, acknowledging the same truth, in silence. It's been an hour since she left, the unopened gift still sitting neatly on my bedside table; my thoughts still dancing with the newly discovered power in my possession. I have spent my entire life being a character in someone else's story. In Mother's story, I am the curse. In Father's story, I am the mistake. Never realizing that I had yet to discover my own story. It was as if a light turned on in my world, illuminating all of the dark corners that I had not yet the years to explore. I would imagine for many children my age, this light comes on slowly and as they grow, the light grows brighter. But for little girls like me, ones with babies growing in their bellies, the light has no patience to wait for length of years.

Ms. Clark arrived not too long after Aunt Susannah's impromptu visit. I can hear her voice faintly coming through the tiny crack in my bedroom door. From the words that I can barely make out, it seems as if she is doing a home inspection with Mother. Probably checking to see how many open bottles of liquor exist in this place. "Baby," I say, looking down at my belly. I had never thought to talk to it before, not quite sure why I was talking to it now. It just felt like, time. "Um," I hesitate, suddenly feeling nervous, shy even, to introduce myself to the life growing inside of me. "Hi. I am your mother." No, that doesn't feel right. "I am your mama. You can even call me that and not mother, if you want? I hope that you're growing real strong in there, and all of the fuss going on in my head earlier didn't disturb you. You just keep on growing and resting okay, and I'll keep you safe, I promise."

"Josephine Dieu, is you talking to yo'self?" Ms. Clark's head came peeking through my door. "Your mother told me where to find your bedroom. It's okay if I come in?" By the time she was done speaking she was already making her way to the side of my bed. I didn't even get a chance to let her know that it was okay for her to enter my room. "Hello, Ms. Clark, pleasure to have you here, ma'am," I say as cordially as I can. A bit of my nervousness coming back from my earlier anticipation of her visit. "You must be sick and tired of laying down. C'mon now get up, and throw some warm clothes on. We going for a walk."

A walk does sound good. I been laying in this bed all week, and for two months prior in a hospital bed, and come to think of it, I was in this bed for two months before I even went to the hospital. "A walk sounds like a wonderful idea, Ms. Clark. Are you sure the doctors won't mind?" I ask, knowing full well that if anybody had my best interest at heart it was this young woman standing next to my bed. "Yes, the doctors don't mind, not one bit, and if they did, well they ain't gotta know everything," She replied, with a wink and a smile.

When the front door opened and that cold wind hit my face, it felt like a kiss straight from the lips of Heaven. For the first time in a long time, I was able to appreciate something. It didn't have to be anything spectacular, although the wind is pretty spectacular. It was just being able to recognize that I was finally a part of this world, able to embrace every gift that it chose to give to me, including this baby. "Well, I ain't never in all my life seen somebody breathe in this cold air with as much love as you," Ms. Clark said, perplexed eyes staring at my face, probably wondering what on earth I was doing. Without even realizing, I was standing, eyes shut tightly, arms stretched out as wide as they could go, feeling as alive as I have ever felt.

"Ready to walk, ma'am?" I say, already five steps ahead of her. The late afternoon sun bringing a welcomed feeling of warmth to my skin. Ms. Clark and I walked all the way to the end of Juniper Trace. Slowly passing all of the homes, filled with neighbors that I myself have never come to know, despite this being the only home that I have ever known. We walk to where the street ends and where the sidewalk of the bustling neighborhood begins, every step in eagerness of the next, barely a word leaving either of our mouths.

As we turn to walk back toward the direction from which we came, Ms. Clark put her hand on my arm, "Why don't we slow down a bit, baby girl. I know you is mighty excited to be out here amongst the living, but you should take it easy on the way back. That, and there is something we need to talk 'bout." I could feel the energy flowing through Ms. Clark's hand straight into my arm. It was nervous energy, something that I had not quite expected a woman with her confidence to possess. "Okay," I answer, sipping slowly from her wealth of nerves, allowing myself to join her. "Josephine, I know what happened to you."

PART FOUR

Spring

29.

Thank-You

Have you ever been held by the earth? She hold on as tight as she can for as long as she can, breathing fresh life into our lungs. She is kind, she is tender, she is real. I lay my body on her body, arms spread out as wide as they could go, no blanket to shield me from the prickly grass underneath my back. I stare up at the sun, only a glance at a time, but long enough to appreciate it for what it is. It's a wonder why we ain't afraid of it? The sun is a giant ball of fire dangling high above our heads, holding on to absolutely nothing. When I hear grown folk talking 'bout love, sometimes I don't think they fully understand it. How can they, with so much pain and hatred going on in the world. If these people truly wanna learn what love is, all they gotta do is look up. The sun know what true love is. It is one of the strongest forces to exist in our universe, and it can destroy us in an instant. Yet, when it come to mama earth, the sun is as gentle as a butterfly resting on a flower. It caresses the surface of her skin with enough heat to warm, and shines just enough light to brighten her darkness. To be loved like the sun love the earth, is what it truly mean to be loved.

The longer I lay in the grass, the more I feel connected to mama earth. Mama told me to do this whenever I'm feeling sad. She say that the best stories to be told are the ones sung by the birds, and told by the wind. All I got to do is listen. I close my eyes and allow my breath to leave my body slowly as I exhale. *Stop thinking and listen to the birds and the wind*, I whisper softly in my mind. Trying to push out thoughts, whether positive or negative ain't easy, especially when your brain run a mile a minute like mine.

These past few months have been stressful on us. Mama and me don't get to spend a lot of time together like we used to, since Christmas and New Year's things been rough. Mama don't tell me much about the things she think I can't handle. She don't want me to worry, especially since my adoption still ain't final yet. I know she having money problems. I heard her telling Miss Felix about something called the stock market and how her money bein' tied up by some rich, white folks. Since then Mama been getting fancied up every day and going out to look for a job, and almost every night she come home and cry. Things just ain't been easy, so I'm doing what Mama said and laying out in the grass, letting mama earth give love to me, like the sun give love to her.

I must have nodded off, not sure for how long, but I was woken up by a voice I ain't recognize. "Excuse me, excuse me, little girl, I'm looking for Clara Pruitt." I open my eyes to see a wrinkly faced white lady staring down at me, not an ounce of kindness living on her expression. "Yes ma'am, that's my mama. She ain't here right now though. Is there something I could do for you?" I say, readjusting to prop myself up on my elbows. "Hmmm," she said as she jotted down her thoughts in a notebook that look similar to Miss Felix's own. "Are you here by yourself?" She asked, pen loaded and ready to fire down whatever response I gave. "Um," I say nervously, this time standing to my feet. "I'm sorry, ma'am, I ain't allowed to talk to no strangers. I gotta get myself in the house." I turned to run as quickly as I could from the stiff-faced lady, unfortunately I wasn't quick enough. She grabbed my arm, not enough to hurt me, but with enough force to get my attention. "Tell your mama that I will be back, girl." With that, she handed me her card, removed her boney fingers from around my arm, and walked off to her car. "

I walked as quickly into the house as I could, not wanting my fear to show. *Who was this lady?* I thought as I stood hiding behind Mama's heavy drapes, peeking through the crack in 'em to make sure the lady actually left. I hope Mama wasn't in no trouble with no stock-market people. I hope they wasn't coming to take what little money she had left. The thoughts flew back and forth across my mind like a ping-pong game, before realizing that in the palm of my hand, crumpled up from my panicked clenching was her calling card. It read, *"Ms. Cathleen Strongberry: DEPARTMENT OF CHILD WELFARE & PROTECTIVE SERVICES."*

30.

Josephine

On the blink of an eye life changes. Ms. Clark calls it "divine order." She says that life is one of those things we are lucky to be a part of, but we do not own it. We cannot buy it, nor can we sell it. Many people tried during slavery, but not even then could one own a life. The body was bought and sold, but the value that exists in a life belongs to no man.

Six months ago, I was a sad, lonely child. Not able to appreciate the life that I was blessed with, because I was made to view myself as a curse. But as I fall deeper in love with the child living inside my belly my perception of everything has changed.

It's like I told Aunt Susannah a couple of months back, the truth always reveals itself. Poor Aunt Susannah, the mere thought of her name brings tears to my eyes. It feels like yesterday, the walk with Ms. Clark up and down the street. I was so afraid that she had discovered my secret. If it were a few days earlier, or perhaps if I were not responsible for this new life, I would have confessed, allowing every bit of my anger to sentence Uncle John to a life of public shame and humiliation. The same humiliation and shame that I felt that night.

My biggest concern now was what Ms. Clark would do with the truth once it was confirmed to her. After all, it was her job to protect children from monsters like Uncle John. But despite my age, I knew that my time for being protected was now shifting into me being the protector. I would never find peace in his arrest, nor would it serve my unborn baby any justice. I understood that by forgiving him I was refusing to carry the burden of his actions with my baby, stripping him of his power over me, and over us. I was no longer afraid of shadows. The only person I knew for sure held my secret was Aunt Susannah. After all, it was her secret too. I knew she was aware of what took place the moment she let me know that her husband was calling out my name in his sleep. It was then that I felt her embarrassment, thick like molasses.

When Ms. Clark presented me with the possible scenario that Uncle John took advantage of me, I neither admitted nor did I deny anything. I continued to enjoy the feeling of the wind as it brushed past my cheeks, listening quietly as she spoke. She did the rest of the talking all the way back to the house. She spoke as if her theory were already confirmed, at one point even saying that Mother was the reason it all came together in her mind.

Apparently Ms. Clark had compiled herself a list of names, which she recited to Mother to gauge her opinion. At the brief mention of Uncle John's name Mother's eyes glazed over, a look Ms. Clark was familiar with based on her experience working other cases like this. It was disturbing to us both that Mother may have known all along, but it was not in the least bit surprising. She would never ruin the good name of her family with a rape scandal.

Eventually we reached the front of the house, where she followed me toward the oak tree where I spent many of my early childhood days sitting under. Watching now, as the wild flowers that live at its base blossom seemingly in front of my very eyes. The same wild flowers that would tickle my feet as I hungrily read as many books as I could fit into my mind.

"Josephine, you have to tell the truth, child." Ms. Clark beginning to look frustrated with my lack of concern over the depth of our one-sided conversation. "Why?" I say, barely an expression on my face, bending over to graze my fingers along the bumpy trunk of the tree, hypnotized by its magnificence. "Because you need to put this man in jail." Her words loud and heavy, bearing the mark of someone who was perhaps seeking justice for crimes done to her. I stop moving, my hands resting flat on the tree, pulling strength from Mother Earth.

"Ms. Clark," I begin, my head bowed in contemplation. My eyes revealing the kind of wisdom that can only be earned from surviving pain. "I spent many years thinking that God didn't listen to me. Most of my time spent crying, wishing that I was never born because nobody wanted me. I thought that I deserved what happened to me that night." I turn my face toward her, tears streaming from my eyes, reaching out to the kindness in hers.

"Come stand here with me, Ms. Clark. I want you to put your hands on this tree trunk, and close your eyes. Close your eyes and look with your heart." She did as I asked, both of us now standing on either side of the grand oak. Eyes shut, both holding on to the tree as if it were the arm of God, connected in a way that the human mind may never fully comprehend. "I want you to see what I see," I say, taking a few breaths before continuing to speak, allowing time for my words to sink in.

Softly, I revealed the only truth that mattered. "Ms. Clark, If I put him in jail, I'm putting my baby in jail. He may have raped my body, but my heart was raped long before. Thing is, I was broken long before there was blood. According to my mother and father I was born broken, but this baby is putting me back together again. Give us a chance, give me a chance to love my child in a way that I have never been loved." With tears rolling down both of our faces, Ms. Clark nodded, not a word able to escape her lips. But I knew in that moment, my baby would always be protected.

31.

Thank-You

What is protection? Does anybody know exactly what that mean? Cuz I is as confused as I ever been 'bout the meaning of a word. When Mama came home I didn't want to tell her 'bout the lady, but despite her stress I knew I had no choice. I fixed dinner for us both, chicken and dumplings. I knew that would put a smile on Mama's face, considering that's her favorite meal in the whole wide world.

I waited until she was done chewing and her plate was clean, before I started speaking. "Mama," I said, putting her hand in mine like she has done with me time and time again. She didn't say anything, her stress starting to show on her face, speeding up the aging process. "We had a visitor today, a lady from Child Protective Services came by looking for you." I paused, took a breath. "I ain't tell her nothing 'bout what going on Mama, I promise. But, she left her card, and she said that she'll be back."

Mama's expression didn't change, her eyes didn't blink, nor did a muscle twitch. "Don't you worry yourself, baby girl. I'm sure it was a routine visit. Maybe your adoption getting ready to be final and they just double-checking things." As she finished her statement, I breathed a sigh of relief and leaned back in my chair, letting the weight that had been sitting on my shoulders melt with the vanilla ice cream and apple pie that I served us for dessert. As we continued eating, the conversation with Mama was barely there, not like it usually is. She ate mostly in silence, only speaking to show appreciation for my hard work in the kitchen. *I would do anything to help Mama, to get her out of whatever mess she is in*, I thought as I watched her glumly eat her pie. I know I ain't know too much 'bout being a grown up, but I know that something had to be done. I had to help my mama; I just didn't know how.

When we was finished up at the table, she excused herself to the front porch. I knew she needed some time to be alone and to rock in her special chair. I was grateful for the time also, because it gave me the space I needed to think. "Think, Thank-You, think!" I said aloud to myself as I washed up the dishes. "Mrs. Dieu," I exclaimed loudly, catching myself as to not disturb Mama. I still have my brave potion. I ain't have time to use it these past couple of months cuz all my focus been on Mama. I can go over to her house, drink my potion, knock on her door, and ask her for a loan. I know she ain't using all that money she got, maybe she would even let me work off whatever I borrow? Maybe this is why I was having all them dreams about my real-life mama taking me to her house, cuz she the one that gonna help me and Mama outta this.

I finished up the rest of my work in the kitchen as quickly as I could before running to my room to make sure that the potion was still tucked safely under my pillow where I left it. *This has got to work*, I thought. I sat at my desk and began writing notes on what exactly I was gonna say to mean, old Mrs. Dieu.

32.

Josephine

"God, thank you for waking me up this morning. Thank you for this baby that is growing inside of me, healthy and strong. Thank you for Mother, protect her today and let her feel love all around. Thank you for Ms. Clark, for the light that shines from her eyes. Amen." I open my eyes, still heavy from sleep. I've been getting myself into the habit of praying right when I wake up in the morning, making sure that I give thanks to God. Even though we didn't always have a great relationship, I'm trying to think of things that I want to pass on to this baby. Things like praying and giving thanks, singing songs, reading books. I'm sure I'll have lots of time to do this when he or she is born, but it's also helping me pass the time as I wait for the special day to arrive.

It's getting closer, I only have about eight weeks left. The hospital has been sending nurses daily, and as the weeks draw closer one may even move in. Ms. Clark says the doctor recommended that I be readmitted into the hospital so they can monitor me more closely, but of course Mother objected. I imagine she is afraid of everyone in the town finding out. I myself, have no idea what absurd story she is going to tell the ladies at Bridge Club when they hear a baby crying during their mid-day cocktails. But, I'm sure whatever she decides to say, it will be entertaining. I yawn loudly as I stretch my arms out in front of me. "What are we going to do today, little one?" I say as my hands rest gently on my belly, amazed at how big it's gotten. "We can sing songs? Draw pictures? Or maybe we can find a new book to read? What do you think?" Before I could make a decision for us both, Mother strolled into my room with a smile on her face, and in very rare form.

"Good morning, Josephine," she said, eyes bright and alarmingly happy. Good morning, Mother. To what do I owe this visit?" I respond, confusion coming through in my tone. "Well, humph! Can I not say good morning to my daughter without having a reason?" she grunted. "I'm sorry, ma'am. I wasn't expecting you. I was just talking to the baby and thinking about drawing or reading a book. You caught me by surprise." I wasn't exactly sure how to respond or react to her. Mother only comes into my room when Ms. Clark is here to put on her show. Besides that, she is a ghost to me, which is something that I am accustomed to. So why now? And with such glee, it's unnatural.

"Well, why don't you read that book Aunt Susannah brought for you? You're so ungrateful you haven't even read it yet?" Book, what book? I think to myself, remembering the gift that Aunt Susannah was carrying on the day of her visit. "Mother, how do you know Aunt Susannah brought me a book?" I asked, unsure of how she knew what it was, and how she knew that I hadn't opened it or read it. "Because she told me, you dumb girl, and I know you haven't read it because I expect no less of an ingrate like you."

I let out a sigh, disappointed that I did not get to enjoy my mother's happy mood for the few moments that it made its presence known. At this point, I am not concerned for me, but for my baby being confined to listen to the mean words that fly out of Mother's mouth. "Is that why you came in here, Mother?" I ask, my energy almost depleted with her presence in my space. "No, I came to tell you that your father's son is dead. Poor child came down with polio or cholera, something like that. Can you believe that?" She said with a smile of contentment, one that sent waves of nausea throughout my body.

I do not understand how cruel one has to be to find joy in the death of another soul, let alone a baby. My heart wrenched for my father, regardless of his opinion of me. Mother walked as casually out of my room as she entered, leaving a bit of darkness in her wake. I said a prayer for the baby brother whom I will never meet, and for his parents who I am sure were distraught. I also said a prayer for my baby, that God would let it live to see a long, healthy, and beautiful life.

How did Mother know that I didn't read the book, I thought to myself again, also wondering where I had even put it. "Oh, yes," I remembered aloud. I stood up slowly, using my arms to propel me forward and off of the bed. I put the gift in my dresser, still wrapped as pretty as it was the day it was placed on my bedside table. I didn't have a desire to open it initially, and soon it became less than a memory.

There it was, underneath a pile of my neatly folded petticoats was the gift. I waddled my very pregnant frame over to the rocking chair in the corner of my bedroom, another gift, except this one from Ms. Clark, and took a seat. I held the small package in my hands, feeling uneasy at the thought of it being from Uncle

John. Yet ashamed at myself for not opening it sooner. It was my pride that was keeping me from accepting this gift, and there is no act of pride which is greater than any act of love.

With that, I allowed myself to begin tearing away at the paper, each piece removed, revealing an image. My hands beginning to tremble as the book shed its covering, *Charlotte's Web*. I put it down in my lap, my hands still trembling as they rested on my belly, positioning them to shield my unborn from a glimpse of its past. Slowly, I rock in my chair. Acknowledging to myself that although I had forgiven, I had not yet forgotten.

33.

Thank-You

"How do you expect to provide for the child that is under your care when you have no money, Ms. Pruitt?" I can feel the tension in the room between Mama and the lady from Child Protective Services, and I'm not even in it. I'm hiding around the corner from where they are sitting in the den, ironically the same den I was sitting in when I found out Mama was going to adopt me. "Listen, Ms. Strongbottom, Strongberry, whatever your name is. That child out there is my baby whether she was born from me or not, and I will do what I have to do to see to it that I can provide for her."

Hearing Mama's voice raised in anger was as unfamiliar as it was unsettling. I'm not sure if it was her tone that caused my knees to shake or the worry that engulfed it. I wasn't sure if Ms. Strongberry believed any of her words, heck, I don't even know if she believed them herself. "Well, Ms. Pruitt, the court's ruling will be in a few weeks to determine if your adoption will be finalized. You have until April to get a steady income coming into your home or that girl out there goes back into the custody of the state." I continued to hide until Ms. Strongberry left. I didn't want Mama to know that I had overheard their conversation. It wouldn't do either of us no good to sit and worry together. I knew what I had to do. It was up to me to help Mama the way she would help me.

I ran into my room, threw on my jacket, and secured my secret weapon which was resting safely under my pillow. With my brave potion now tucked snuggly in my pocket, I ran past Mama who was making her way to the kitchen. "Bye, Mama. I got something for Mrs. Dieu. I'll be back before it get dark. I love you." I didn't even give her a chance to respond before my skinny little legs were out the front door.

I walked most of the way, allowing time for my mission to play and replay itself in my mind. It was as if I were a spy from a secret military office sent to save the world. I knew what needed to be done, and I was prepared to do it. I had to get Mrs. Dieu to not only open her front door, but also speak to me, and convince her to let the strange little girl who leaves her presents borrow money to save her family.

It all seemed simple enough, or so I'd hoped. I wasn't quite sure how it would all come together, but that didn't matter. I knew that it would work itself out, because I had faith. I been learning 'bout faith all my life. Miss Felix taught me that faith is one of humanity's most powerful gifts. It not only means believing in things you can't see, but it acts as the foundation for each individual's purpose in life to not only be recognized, but fulfilled. It is the flame that lights the match, which sets our purpose on fire. I can hear Miss Felix voice now: "Faith shine a big light on purpose, baby girl. The amount of faith you put in something, tell you how much that thing worth to you, and whatever mean the most, well that's how you get to figuring out what your purpose is."

As I approached Juniper Trace, I was reminded of my first visit. The first time my lips sounded out the words to the street sign, and remembered how my blood ambushed my veins causing my thoughts to spiral into a frenzy. Today was gonna be different. I am not afraid this time, because I have my brave potion. And above all else I have faith that I was meant to have a real-life family.

I stopped walking as my eyes caught sight of the familiar oak tree. I took a moment to prepare myself, carefully removing the vial from its holding place in my pocket. I unscrewed the top with precision as if I had done this one hundred times before and pressed the small glass container to my lips, swallowing its contents with one little gulp. The taste on my tongue lingering for more than a few moments, sending all types of messages to my taste receptors. "Mmmm," I said aloud, it tasted like sugar, green apples, and cinnamon. *Mama sure does know how to make a good potion*, I thought, as my feet hurried themselves toward the house of the infamous Dieu family.

I had no time today to pick or play with wildflowers. I needed to get this over with before the potion wore off. I got up on the porch and wasted no time knocking on the door. Silently debating with myself whether or not I should have rung the bell, since that's more polite. *No, polite was not the way to go*, I thought as I knocked again. I needed this mean old lady to know that I was here on official business. Maybe if she took me seriously she would be more keen on helping us. *Knock knock knock knock knock knock knock.* At this point my hands felt like they were playing some sort of exotic musical instrument.

"Hello, is anybody home?" I yelled bravely at the grand double doors. Just as I was getting discouraged I heard a creak. The doors were opening, slowly, but they were opening. I felt no nerves, no anxiety, just waves of bravery crashing along the shore in my mind, "Mrs. Dieu!" I exclaimed. There was no response, just the steady creak of the door. I waited, my patience being tested like a raging bull staring at a red cloth, my breathing heavy in anticipation. The doors opened, revealing a face that I did not expect to see.

34.

Josephine

"Does life happen to us? Or, does life happen for us?" I asked a confused-looking Ms. Clark. She peered at me, unsure of how to answer my array of questions. For a young woman, she is wise beyond her years. Her influence on my own mind has been invaluable. She has taught me to question things about life, God, and family. Things that I never thought to question before. "Well, I think the answer gonna be different for each of us, depending on how it is we look at life," she said softly. I knew she was gonna give me that response, but I had already figured that part out. What I wanted to know was how she viewed it.

"Well, how do you look at life, Ms. Clark?" Her eyes shifted, she took her gaze off of me and focused on her hands. "Life does happen for me." She paused, shifting her brown eyes back to me. "I think if we let it, it can happen for all of us. Everything that happen, whether good or bad, serve its purpose. The people that say life happen to them, those the people that feel powerless, those the ones that ain't got their eyes open to the big picture of things." Contentment spread across her face as she concluded her statement. I knew her and I shared the same belief on life, and she knew it too. "So what do you think I should do about the book?" I asked, bringing back the reason I started asking questions in the first place.

I wanted to read *Charlotte's Web*, yet, every time I picked it up I felt heavy. I knew that by not allowing myself to read it, I was still holding on to things that I needed to let go of. I just didn't yet know how. I was hoping that Ms. Clark would be able to give me some insight, considering there was nothing that I didn't tell her. Since the day we held on to that tree trunk together, I knew that she was on my side. "Well, I think you should close your eyes, and look with your heart," she said as she winked. "Somehow you always know what I'm thinking," I said as we both giggled. She was right, I needed to take a step back and decide with my heart, and I had a feeling I already knew what I was going to do.

I was way too pregnant to see Ms. Clark out. This baby had grown so big inside of my belly, it was a wonder it wasn't already walking and talking yet. As I heard her say goodbye to Mother, I reached for the book which she cunningly placed on my bedside table before she left. I could only smile to myself at how well she knew me, letting the thought of her friendship warm my heart. "Okay, little flower," I said out loud. "It's story time."

I held the book in both hands, brought it up to my face, and drew in it's scent. I have always loved the smell of books, and this one would be no different. This was simply another part of the healing process. It's time to let it all go. I wasn't sure how it would feel to skim my eyes along the familiar pages, and begin to read the story that came alive in my dreams that night in the bookshop. I was afraid that by bringing the story alive again, that I would bring along with it everything that occurred. But that's not what happened. With my conversation with Ms. Clark settling into the back of my mind I began to read out loud to my baby. With every word that escaped my lips I took back each second that was stolen from me. I read and cried, I read, and healed.

The process of healing has been a long one. One in which so many people never see to the end. This was my end. I consider myself one of the lucky ones, able to grow as the flower inside me grows. I read for hours, losing track of time. Not eating the meal that was placed in front of me by one of the maids. Barely noticing the nurse that came to check on me before she left for the night. I read, and reread the book until I fell asleep, until it's words became etched into my soul and the lives of the characters intertwined with my own.

35.

Thank-You

"Yes, can I help you?" The young lady spoke, her voice mesmerizing. I wasn't sure how to respond. I was preparing my words for Mrs. Dieu, but this clearly wasn't her. "I'm sorry to bother you, ma'am, I'm looking for Mrs. Dieu. Is she home?" Instead of giving me a response, the lady invited me inside. I wasn't sure if Mama would be upset with me for following her in, but this is what I'd been dreaming 'bout. This was the moment in my dreams where the light would burst through the doors, engulfing me in eternal brightness.

I squinted my eyes when I walked in, just in case my dream became reality, but no such thing happened. There was no bright illuminating light. There was nothing but an old dusty, musty smelling house. "Would you like something to drink?" The lady asked. "No, thanks," I replied as politely as I could. My eyes couldn't believe how the wealthy Dieu family was living. The house was a mess. The furniture hadn't been properly dusted in what seemed like years, and there were dirty dishes and garbage everywhere. If it weren't for my curiosity, I would have run home the minute I walked in.

"So what is it you want with my mother?" the lady asked. The light from an open window shining on her face, revealing beauty unlike any I had ever seen. Immediately I could see the resemblance that she shared with Mrs. Dieu. They shared the same cinnamon skin tone, as well as the same cluster of freckles under their eyes. I couldn't take my eyes off of her, and she awkwardly noticed. "Little girl, are you okay?" she said again. She wasn't being mean. I understand how strange I must have seemed. First, I knocked on her door over and over again. Then, I come into her house and stare at her, words unable to detach themselves from my tongue. "I, um, I was hoping that I could ask her a question, ma'am." I managed to stammer after countless seconds of immobile staring.

She took a heavy gulp of air, almost like a sigh, just a bit more intense. "I'm sorry to have to tell you this, but my mother is no longer with us." Her sadness turned to bewilderment as she witnessed the tears fall from my eyes. "She's dead," I said, unable to stop the sorrow that filled my heart for the mean, old lady. "Oh no, I'm sorry, no, she's not dead. She has been sent to live in an assisted-care facility up north. She can be taken care of there. She has a disease called Alzheimer's, which means she has no memories of her life, not even of me."

As she continued to speak my eyes were intoxicated by each movement she made with her mouth. The tone of her voice was one in which I had heard before, I knew this woman. "I didn't realize Mother had any friends though? May I ask how you know her?" Her question interrupting my intoxication. I thought quickly, wondering if my brave potion was still in effect. How was I gonna explain everything that had been going on since the day I came to live with Miss Clara. I decided it would be best to give the short version. "Well, ma'am, I don't exactly know your mama. I just been visiting her for a few months since I started my reading lessons over by y'all library. I been making her presents and leaving them out by the front door, hoping that she was getting them and the love I made them with. She seemed awfully lonely ma'am, and that made my heart sad for her."

The young lady stared at me. The look in her eyes carefully guarding her thoughts. For a moment I thought she was gonna cry. I thought she was gonna breakdown and release whatever animosity she had toward her mama. Even though she seemed to be kind, there was a sadness in her eyes that I almost didn't catch. "Well, Mother was lucky to have you as a neighbor. Were you coming to leave something for her today?" she asked, her voice stifled as if holding back a wealth of emotion. "No ma'am. To be quite honest, I was coming by today to ask your mama for a loan. Please don't tell my mama, cuz she gonna be real vex with me if she find out. Things just been real tough lately cuz my mama ain't the one that I fell out of. She my adopted mama, but the mean-faced social worker, Ms. Strongberry, say she gonna take me away unless my mama got money again, and I was gonna pay your mama back when we get all this settled and we become a family."

I wasn't prepared to tell all that truth, but that's what my teeth wanted cuz that's what came out. I stood waiting for a response, a reply of any sort, but for more than a few moments there was silence. I could tell that she was processing my words, trying to figure out what kind of person I was before she spoke. "Hmm, I'm so sorry for that, and my mother isn't in any position to be able to help you. Don't worry about me speaking to anyone about this, I'm not going to be here for long. I just came to clean up my mother's things so I can sell the house. But, if you're interested in helping, perhaps I can hire you to give me a hand?" I was so excited, I let out a high-pitched, "Really?" I knew there was a reason I was having all those dreams. "I would love to, ma'am. Thank you so much." After arranging to meet Miss Dieu at noon the next day, I headed for the door. "I'm sorry, little girl, I didn't catch your name." I stopped, and looked up at my new boss showing her all of my teeth. "Thank-You, ma'am. My name is Thank-You.

36.

Josephine

As much as I loved the name Charlotte for a girl, it saddened me to think that she dies in the book. *Do I really want to name my baby after such a tragic character?* I wonder to myself. Rocking slowly in my chair, writing possible baby names down in a notebook gifted to me by Ms. Clark. The only names I have so far in my collection are Fern and Charlotte for a girl, and Wilbur for a boy. It's no surprise that those are the only names that have been repeating themselves in my mind for a week. I have to come up with new names, give myself options. "Thomasina," I say aloud. *Yuck*, I think. I've got to do better than that. Clark for a boy would be nice, and that would make Miss Clark feel really special, I think as I write the name down.

"Josephine," I hear mother's voice penetrate through my walls. *Will she ever stop yelling*, I wonder. I usually don't respond to her anymore. It is highly probable that she is yelling my name to forewarn me that I have a doctor arriving for a visit. There has been some concern about the baby, and Mother is still refusing to have me admitted into the hospital. I would run away and carry myself, but I can't run. All I can do is focus on having a healthy baby, and I've been doing all I can to make sure that happens. I've been praying, eating right, and trying to walk back and forth to my rocking chair as often as I can. Anything the doctors and nurses tell me to do, I do.

"Josephine," I hear mother's voice from outside of my door. "It's open," I say. "Ah, there she is," mother says as she opens my door, looking first toward my bed where I'm not laying, then over to the rocking chair. "Josephine, this is Doctor Robinson. He is going to be your new doctor, and his nurse will replace the one sent by the hospital. Do you understand?" Her face was stern as usual, not showing any sense of warmth. "Yes, ma'am, I understand. But the doctors in the hospital are already familiar with me and my case." I replied, perplexed. "How dare you disrespect this nice man that has traveled all the way from New York to stay with us and deliver your bastard child. I only hired him so that you would get the best care possible, and this is the thanks I get?" The doctor stood behind Mother, his face as cold as hers. I felt embarrassed for my initial response and apologized to them both, although it still didn't feel right.

I lay still as I let Doctor Robinson do his examination. He checked my pulse, my temperature, my blood pressure, and rubbed his fat sweaty palms over my belly a few times. In my past experience doctors had always worn gloves, but not this one. Not only did he not wear gloves, but he didn't yet have a nurse to accompany him. Instead, he had Mother standing in the room to bear witness that he was only looking and touching what he was supposed to. "Mrs. Dieu," he spoke to Mother as if she were the one having the baby. "I don't like the looks of things. We may have to do something to have this baby come along faster." "What?" I interjected. Making clear to him that I was the one that would be bringing this new life into the world, and not my mother. She was just the one signing his paycheck.

"What do you mean, sir, about bringing the baby along faster?" I felt a bit of my mother's temper come out of me, something that I didn't even know I was in possession of. "We may not have a choice Miss Dieu, if you want this baby born alive." The doctor's words put tears in my eyes, as if he had placed them there himself. Of course I wanted my baby to be born alive, anything else wasn't even an option. I hadn't even thought about the possibility of losing this baby, my baby. I would do whatever it takes to keep it safe, even if it meant trusting this doctor.

37.

Thank-You

I ran all the way home, barely stopping to catch my breath. The excitement of what had just taken place was rushing through my mind. I could barely contain my thoughts any longer. I wanted to stop and tell every squirrel that I saw scurry by, hoping that one of them would be like my old friend Grandma and listen to my stories. When I got home, Mama was still sitting on the front porch rocking in her chair.

"Mama," I proclaimed, happy as a bear in a beehive. As I was about to ramble off the day's news, I realized that by telling her everything I would have to tell her that I went to Mrs. Dieu's house to ask for a loan. I knew that she would have been disappointed and more than anything else, I knew that she would have been embarrassed. "Baby girl, why you looking like you was just handed over a candy store?" I stopped, forcing the smile on my face to disappear. I knew that for right now, this was a secret that I had to keep until I made enough money to confess.

Knowing that I could not tell a convincing lie, I embellished on the truth, just a bit. "Oh, well when I left the Dieu's house I passed by so many squirrels. I was just remembering how much I loved them, and wanted to share it with you." I held my breath for a second or two, not sure if Mama believed me, but she trusted that I wouldn't tell a lie again. But, this time was different. This time, Mama was doing the same thing. She wasn't telling me the truth 'bout what was going on either. We were both doing what we thought needed to be done to save our family.

The only thing I had to figure out was what to tell Mama I would be doing with my days. I couldn't lie and tell her I was going to the library because Mister Clarence would never lie to Mama for me. I could tell her that I was spending my days at the Dieu's house. That wouldn't be a lie. I simply wouldn't go into the details of the story, nor would I tell her which one of the Dieu's I would be spending my time with. I know she would assume it was Mrs. Dieu since no one ever mentioned her having a daughter.

The next morning, I jumped out of bed. I must have flown so high my head barely missed the ceiling. I made my bed as quickly as I could, making sure that I didn't make much noise as to not wake Mama. I wanted to surprise her with breakfast, and also get my reading work done so that she would let me leave by noon. Just because I ain't in school yet, don't mean that I get to do whatever I please. My mama is the sweetest, kindest mama that anybody would ever ask for, but when it come to reading, writing, and arithmetic she don't play.

I get myself ready for the day and hustle my little butt to the kitchen to prepare a meal fit for a queen. What I found instead, broke my heart. She must not have had enough money to go to the market, and all we had for breakfast was a couple of stale slices of bread and one egg. I should have been paying more attention to this. I should have known, Mama always make the best meals, and lately she been cooking whatever she could find. She been going through this all on her own, and here I been stuck in my own world.

The contents of the pantry solidified my decision to work with Miss Dieu in secret to help Mama. I toast and butter up the last two slices of bread, and fry the egg up for Mama, just like she like. I knew that she would want to see me fed before she allowing herself to eat, so I kept one slice of toast for myself.

I walked into her room carrying a tray adorned with her breakfast, toast, an egg, and a small cup of tea. And to make her smile, yellow moonbeam flowers in a small vase, which I freshly borrowed from mama earth for the occasion. "Mama, I hope you're hungry," I say as I walk gingerly into her room. "Baby girl, what is you doing up so early?" she asked, half asleep, readjusting herself to sit up in the bed. "I made you breakfast, Mama. I wanted to surprise you." Her eyes sparkled, showing delight for her early morning surprise. I put the tray down in front of her and gave her a kiss on the cheek.

I didn't know if things was gonna work out for me and Mama. I don't think Mama knew either. All we had was hope, and the desire to be a family. When I moved in with her all them months back, we didn't know how badly we needed each other. We was both yearning for that feeling of completeness that only a family could give you, and for the first time we was getting a taste of it. Mama was getting a taste of it with every bite she took out that toast. Every bite tasted like love.

38.

Josephine

A mother is to her unborn child as God is to us, that invisible force that keeps us protected and safe. We may not see it, but we know that something is holding on to us, breathing new life into us daily. To my unborn baby I am God, and to my God I am an unborn baby. At times we fail to realize that we do not merely exist on this earth, but we exist in this earth. She is like a mother carrying us within her womb, nourishing us with her body. My job as a mother is to see my unborn baby safely journey from my womb, into the womb in which we will explore together.

"What is the matter, baby girl?" I hear Ms. Clark's voice, and although I want to respond, I simply cannot find the words. "I been sitting here for over an hour staring at you, and you ain't said but five words to me. I need to know what it is, so I can help you, Josephine." How was I to explain to Ms. Clark what I was feeling, when she herself has never experienced a life growing inside of her. "Ms. Clark, my new doctor said that if I don't let them take out my baby early, it may not survive. They want to do it soon." The words trickled out of my mouth slowly before turning into huge gasping sobs. "My baby can die."

Ms. Clark walked over and sat next to me on the bed. She took my head and rested it on her chest. I inhaled her scent, her perfume sweetly embracing my nose as she quietly rocked me back and forth. "Please don't let nothing happen to my baby," I whisper, unsure if I were speaking to Ms. Clark, or to God. We sat like that for about thirty minutes, her arms wrapped around me, steadily rocking as my tears seeped into her blouse. Teaching me that one does not need to carry a child to experience what it is to be a mother, nor does one need that credential to be good at it.

"Let me go talk to your mama and find out exactly what this new big-shot doctor talking 'bout." Before getting up, she kissed me right in the middle of my forehead, a place I had never been kissed before. I made a mental note to always kiss my baby in that spot, where the heart meets the eyes.

I listened as best as I could to Ms. Clark's voice as it met with Mother's somewhere down the stairs. I could make out bits and pieces of their conversation, each one going back and forth about what the best options were for me and the baby. I heard Ms. Clark say that I should have been taken to a hospital, and not hidden in a room like some whore. Insinuating to Mother that she was aware of her knowledge of how I came to have this baby inside of me. I listened until I did not want to hear anymore. It was all too much. They were out there arguing while my baby's life was at stake. I picked up *Charlotte's Web* and began to read aloud, closing my eyes and reciting my favorite parts by memory.

I didn't get the chance to finish the book this time. Nor did I realize that it would be the last time that my eyes would breathe in the lives of Wilbur, Fern, and Charlotte. How interesting, when I think on it now. I died my first death reading a book about just that; death.

The pain rose up from my abdomen like nothing I had ever experienced or could ever describe. Words were not an option, but from inside of my mind I could hear the scream that liberated itself from my lungs. I could hear Ms. Clark and Mother's feet pounding up the stairs as Mother yelled for the doctor. We all knew what was happening. The journey had begun.

39.

Thank-You

It felt like death. Every room that I went into was dark and gloomy. Dust and cobwebs claimed ownership of tables, chairs, dishes, carpets, books, and drapes. Nothing was spared from the invasion of darkness that lived here, making no room available for even a glimmer of light to enter. How could anybody live like this? It seemed impossible that a human bean had lived here in this darkness, but Mrs. Dieu did. That's why they had to send her away, because she became as the darkness was. Her mind an empty room covered in dust and cobwebs.

It saddened me to think that I would never get to know her. I had been so fascinated with her for so many months, even in my dreams. The fantasy in my mind of befriending her was overshadowed by the reality of who she really was. A puzzle which I had begun to put together the longer I helped her daughter clean, pack, and throw away her belongings. There were no family photo albums, no pictures in frames hanging on any of the multitude of walls. There was nothing indicating that she had any warmth in her heart, because there was none in her home.

When I first arrived to help Miss Dieu I was overtaken by the situation, so much so that I was not much of a conversationalist. I did as she asked me to do, working carefully behind her so that I would not get in her way. She was soft-spoken and polite, busying herself to get the task at hand done as quickly as possible. Although she did not speak much, it was clear that I felt more comfortable being in her mama's home than she did. We stayed on the first floor of the house for most of the day, strangers connected by a single thread of commonality. We were both here, doing this for our mamas.

"Excuse me, Miss Dieu, ma'am, how come you ain't sad 'bout yo mama?" I asked, finally breaking the silence. She looked at me from across the room as she was in the middle of wiping the dust off of a bunch of fancy plates and cups. "I'm sorry, what did you ask? I'm not used to being called Miss Dieu. You can call me Josephine," she responded, the look in her eyes giving away that she heard my question, but wasn't prepared to answer. So I asked again, this time referring to her as Josephine and elevating my voice so that it carried itself slowly across the room giving her time to prepare a proper response. "Well, it's not that I'm not sad. My mother and I just weren't close, and I haven't seen her in many years." She took in a deep breath, her voice dropping low, "I guess I'm not that sad after all." She continued wiping down her china showing no signs that she wanted to continue on with the conversation.

I wasn't sure what to do. I was here to work and make money for Mama, but I still wanted to understand why this house and this family made me feel so strange. The only person who could

166

answer my questions went ahead and forgot all of the answers, and her daughter probably didn't know much or at least that's what she was letting on. Or maybe I just wasn't asking the right questions? I thought carefully before I spoke for a second time. "Did you like growing up around these parts, ma'am?" I asked, making every effort to get the nice young lady to start talking. She looked up at me again, this time she was in the middle of wrapping all that fancy glassware into newspaper and putting them gently into a box marked "*Fine China.*"

"It was okay," she replied. She must have felt my disappointment in receiving such a short response, and gave in to the musings of a little girl. "It was great. There is a big oak tree out front that I would lay under and read my books, the wind would graze past my cheeks and make me blush at its tenderness, bringing with it the smell of gardenias straight from Heaven." Her words began to flow from her as beautifully as sound flows from a violin. Her eyes drifting off in remembrance of her time spent on Juniper Trace, forgetting that she was speaking to a stranger. "I loved riding my bike around the neighborhood, smelling the fresh-baked pies, waving hello to strangers." I listened intently, reminding myself to not interrupt her as she spoke as to not break her concentration. She seemed happy to speak of her time here, to share with me a bit of who she was.

"So tell me, Thank-You, since we're being frank with each other. How did your mother come up with such a peculiar name?" Her question causing a smile to spread across her face, sending those ole familiar goose pimples racing up and down my body. I have never been known to get tongue tied, or to be at a loss for words, but something 'bout that smile changed my life. I was trying so hard to speak I stammered on the first few words "Mi-i-sss

D-dd-ieu, mm-ma'am, I can, I can only tell you what I been told. When my mama was having me she so grateful for me that that's what she called me. I ain't never been able to confirm whether or not that was the real reason cuz she dd-dead, ma'am, and I ain't never had no daddy."

Josephine's gaze was fixed on me, this time with a look in her eyes that I had seen before, revealing her innocence. The thing with death is, everyone that has experienced the loss of a loved one gets the same look in their eyes when the topic is brought up. It is a look that encompasses empathy, understanding, and a glimpse of their own grief despite how long it had been since their loved one passed. It was clear, that she had lost someone that she loved.

"I'm sorry to hear that you've experienced so much pain in this life already. You know, you and I probably aren't so different, Thank-You. By the time I was your age I felt like I was an old woman. I wish that I had your charisma back then. I'm sure your mother would be very proud of you. I know I would be." Her words brought comfort to my spirit, I had often wondered if my mama was proud of me, and hearing a stranger say that she would be proud if she was my mama made me feel really good.

40.

Josephine

"Josephine Dieu, you better not go nowhere, do you hear me? You better stay with me and have this baby. We come too far, baby girl!" The sound of Ms. Clark's voice floated in and out of my ears as I floated in and out of consciousness. I wasn't ready to have this baby; my body wasn't ready. I felt as if I was yelling, "I'm not ready," to the world, to Mother, and Ms. Clark, but no one heard me. The words were unable to pass from my lips as they turned blue, cold with the amount of blood that I was losing. I knew that I could feel pain, my body swallowed by it, engulfing my stomach in flames. I would fight for my baby. I had to fight for my baby.

I felt my face wet with tears, sweat, water from a rag that Ms. Clark was gently resting on my forehead as each contraction took hold of my body by force. In all of those baby books Ms. Clark gave me to read, no one ever mentioned that childbirth felt like a steam engine was going to barrel its way through my body, threatening to not only take the baby but every vital organ that my body needed to sustain itself. "Be strong, baby girl, be strong." Ms. Clark's voice cut through the pain a little at a time, comforting what it could. I wanted to make her proud. I wanted to show her what a good mother I was going to be. My baby was going to call me "Mama" and it was going to be the love of my life. I wanted to be strong so that my baby would know what strength felt like.

"Doctor, do something. That's too much blood! Where the hell is Mrs. Dieu?" I have never heard Ms. Clark panic like that before. If I had time to worry I may have started then. *Where was Mother?* I briefly thought, knowing that it was best she stayed out of the room. I preferred to have Ms. Clark with me anyway. "This baby is coming whether or not we are ready for it," the doctor's voice booming over Ms. Clark's, dominating my screams. "Josephine, I need you to push when I tell you to." I followed the sound of his voice with my eyes. Fighting to keep them open as they filled with water, getting heavier with each passing second. I still didn't trust this doctor, but what choice did I have? My baby chose to come now. If he said push, then I pushed. I knew that Ms. Clark would never let anything happen to me or my baby.

"Push," his voice knocking the wind out of me. I was trying with all my might, my world going in and out of fuzziness. Where was Ms. Clark? I tried to call for her, but I had no voice myself. I had no idea how many minutes had passed since I'd heard the sound of her voice, cheering me on, giving me hope. *Where did you go, Ms. Clark?* I asked in my mind, hoping that she would hear me. "Baby girl, stay with us now, your mama gonna stand beside you and help you." She was back, but to tell me that she was leaving me to do this on my own with Mother. "Ya'll need each other now, baby girl".

Her voice was that of an angel, but the words she spoke brought no peace to my spirit. With every extra ounce of strength I could afford to take from my unborn baby I turned my face toward Ms. Clark, passing over Mother's as she stood ready to take Ms. Clark's place next to my bed. Whether it was divine grace, or instincts, I knew that it would be the last time that my eyes were to rest on her.

In this moment I saw Ms. Clark for all that she was. She was the most beautiful person that I have ever laid eyes upon. Her body wrapped in a soft, warm glow, ready to wrap me in its arms. By the way that I looked at her she knew that I did not want her to go, and she also knew that I was saying goodbye.

With my gaze still fixed on Ms. Clark, I watched the tears as they streamed down her cheeks. She walked slowly, backwards out of the room as Mother told the nurse to lead her out. Our eyes holding on for every second that they were allowed, watching each other as we heard the sound that made every negative moment in the world disappear.

There is nothing like hearing the sound of your baby for the first time. It is the closest thing to hearing what Heaven's choir sounds like from the front row. It may seem silly, describing a cry as heavenly, but oh, it's as sweet as any symphony that could be sung by any angel bringing with it the scent of gardenias that must have crept through a crack in my bedroom window.

Although I would never get the chance to hold it in my arms, or kiss the middle of its forehead like I'd wished, my baby sang to me the sweetest song that I had ever heard. It sang to me a lullaby of love, filling my spirit with peace. With the end of my life resting on my lips and my eyes still resting on Ms. Clark, I whispered, "thank you," to my God, to Ms. Clark, and to my baby. It was through them, I was made whole. My body went limp as she was pulled out of the room, my "thank you" resonating deep within her spirit.

PART FIVE

Present Day

41.

Thank-You

Everybody got a story. It don't matter who you is or where you come from, as long as you got breath in yo body you got a story to tell. The more people start sharing they stories the faster we gonna learn to appreciate each other, and recognize how similar we all is. Every human bean is connected to the other, despite the color they was born wearing or the language they was born speaking. We is all brothers, sisters, fathers, and daughters of the same universe, eating from the same table of life, drinking from the same well of knowledge. We experience the same array of emotions and are all on the path searching for the same thing. We is all searching for love, in any way that it make sense to us.

Standing in the Dieu house reminds me of so many foster homes I done been in. So many of them were a glimmer of light in the beginning, allowing hope to grow in my heart before eventually turning into darkness, pulling out my hope like a gardener pull weeds out from around a rose bush. Every day I come here I think of them dreams I had 'bout that burst of light engulfing me, yet every time I come all I find waiting for me is darkness. I been working with Josephine for almost two weeks, and our time together just about done. She been real kind to me, and always telling me how grateful she is for my help. But this poor thing got something living on the inside of her that almost as dark as the house.

At first, I thought the darkness was coming from the energy that her mama left behind, but I'm beginning to realize that she brought in a bit of her own. I'm not sure if I'm meant to do anything to help her, or if I'm best just keeping my thoughts to myself. Perhaps the only thing that I can do is stay quiet, make my money, and use all my energy to save me and Mama from Ms. Strongberry. But Miss Felix always taught me that you should always pay attention to the signs that life give you. "Ain't nothing a coincidence," she say, her voice echoing in my ears.

So why is I here now? I thought to myself as I made my way from room to room checking to see what else needed to be done. I walked up and down the first floor hallway, peeking in rooms we done cleaned, listening to hear Josephine's voice just in case she needed me to help her with something. She gave me instructions to only work on the first floor, saying that she could handle the second floor of the house. But it seem as though my hard work done paid off and all my rooms is done. All the cobwebs is gone, the stuff packed in boxes, leaving only shadows to play with the memories of what once existed.

"Josephine," I called out from the bottom of the stairs. I was greeted with no response, as I permitted myself to take one step up. There was a slight groan on the wooden staircase as it met with my small feet. "Josephine," I said, this time speaking a bit louder. Still not a sound coming to me from the second floor of the house. I decided to take a few more steps, this time not speaking, only listening for the sounds of movement. *She must be real busy up there*, I thought to myself as I continued moving upward on the staircase. I didn't think she would be upset with me if I invited myself to the second floor, my intentions were honest and simple. To make as much money as I could and to help as much as I could.

I reached the second level, which was astonishingly darker than the first. The dust filled my lungs as I made my way down a long, dreary hallway. There was barely any opening for light to stream in, and a layer of heaviness coated the bare walls as if years of secret keeping finally took their toll. "Josephine," I whispered, my voice refused to come out any louder. The house felt haunted. I remembered Mister Clarence's words all of those months back at the library. He said that someone had died in their family, and I never found out who it was. Maybe whoever it was, died here, in this house? The thought causing every hair that was attached to my body to stand upright as if ready to make their escape.

My breath was heavy as I walked, the little voice inside my head was getting louder, telling me it was time to turn around. I almost did, before I heard the sound of someone crying. It sounded like a little girl, my age or younger. I wasn't sure where it was coming from, but my feet were moving against my better judgment in its direction. It was as if I were in a trance, the sound was familiar yet terrifying considering that I was in a strange place. The sound led me to a door which was almost completely shut, except for a small stream of sunlight which was sneaking its way in through a crack. I thought of knocking, but I was too afraid. Instead, I approached the door and slowly pushed it open.

Sitting curled up on the floor was Josephine. Her hands were clutching something tightly to her body, legs pushed up to her chest as she was sobbed silently and uncontrollably. "Josephine," I whispered as not to startle her. She looked up at me, first with embarrassment in her eyes, and then relief. I wasn't sure what I was supposed to do. Miss Felix's words were playing themselves over in my mind. This is why I was here, because she needed me, and God didn't want her to be alone. I walked over to her and sat next to her on the floor, stretching my little arm as far as it could go around her body. She felt my concern and my warmth as she allowed her body to relax into mine. I held her as she cried, knowing that my words would bear no comfort, I didn't say a word.

I held her for what seemed like hours. The sun which once hung high up in the sky was now making its slow decline to kiss mama earth goodnight. "Josephine, ma'am, whatever it is, it gonna be okay," I spoke, once again breaking the silence that had become a familiar part of our relationship. I brushed back the few strands of hair that had matted themselves to her forehead, a reminder of how hot it was in the house. She stirred a bit, and I realized that she was asleep. As much as I didn't want to move her, I had to get home before Mama got worried about me. I began to slowly reposition myself so that I could prop her up against the bed which I was leaning on. As I moved her, the mysterious object which she had been holding on to dislodged itself from her arms, falling next to my leg. Moving with ease I used my free arm to pick it up. "*Charlotte's Web*," I softly read aloud.

"Read it to me," she spoke softly. Awakened by the sound of my words, her voice hoarse from her earlier sobs. "Please," she spoke again. I knew that Mama would be upset with me for staying out past supper, but something in me couldn't leave here, not like this. I wriggled my left arm from around her back, her head repositioning itself to rest on my shoulder as I opened the book to page one.

I allowed my eyes to fixate on each word, giving each one time to roll off of my tongue with the respect that it deserved. In the months since I'd learned to read I had fallen deeper and deeper in love with words. But these words, they were different. One might even say magical. As I read them aloud, they began to come alive right before my eyes. It was as if I had heard this story one million times before, feeling as though I wasn't even reading. I was reciting the words from a place hidden deep within my memory. These characters felt like old friends. I knew them and they knew me.

She rested against my shoulder as we journeyed together through the dreamlike world that opened up before us. In this moment we were infinite, the night was no longer dark. The heaviness was lifting itself as if we were lifting with it. The light that existed in my dreams began to spill itself out of the pages, filling the room with its magnificence. "Josephine," I whispered, wondering if she was experiencing this too. I looked over at her, my eyes filling with tears as they connected with hers, her face was turned toward mine, reflecting my own. She moved nearer to me, I felt her breath on my face as her soft lips pressed themselves against the center of my forehead right between my eyes. In that moment I felt our hearts connect, and our spirits became as one. It was then that I knew, Josephine was not a stranger to me. It was her blood that was running through my veins, and her light that was shining through my eyes.

Uncertain if we were dreaming, I chose not to question it. I was not afraid of what was happening; it was as if we had transcended this life into another. A life in which she was my real-life mama and I was her real-life baby girl. Able to hold each other, and breathe each other in. I will never forget what she smells like. Like fresh gardenias growing wild like fire along fences and up trees, spreading themselves like much-needed truth in a world full of lies. She slowly pulled her face away from mine, her eyes shining like golden amber orbs, her face no longer that of a young woman, her true identity revealing itself to be a girl no older than me. "Thank-You, continue to look with your heart and your days will be as bright as your dreams. You are not a seeker of the light, my sweet girl, you are the light. I loved you before I met you, and we will meet again." Her words were spoken in a way that did not require movement from her lips, we were communicating through God.

42.

Thank-You

I do not know the point in which I fell asleep. I was awoken by the sound of banging on the front door. *Thump thump thump.* I jumped up, my heart suddenly racing, realizing that I was still on the floor. "Oh, no," I said out loud. "Josephine," I called out for Miss Dieu. It must have been my mama at the door coming to look for me. *I'll find her later*, I thought as I ran as quickly as I could down the stairs. I opened the door to find a panic stricken Mama and Miss Felix who appeared to be in worse shape.

"Mama," I said aloud. "I am so sorry. I fell asleep reading a story last night." She hugged me so tight I thought we was gonna combust. Miss Felix stood still, not speaking a word. "Baby girl, I was worried sick. I called Felix and told her we had to find you. I thought the worst had happened to my baby, and I didn't know what to do with myself," Mama spoke as her tears made their way on to her cheek. I knew she loved me, I could feel it so strong coming through her body as she held me.

"Felix, thank God we found her," Mama said turning her attention to the silent Miss Felix who was standing next to her. She didn't respond, the look on her face indicating that she was lost in her thoughts. "Felix," Mama said again, this time loudly to get her attention. She looked at Mama, then at me, her jaw slightly hanging open. "Thank-You, what is you doing here?" she asked, her voice filled with confusion and astonishment. I reminded her of the old lady I was bringing gifts to, the one that was mean and never opened her door when I knocked. It had been some months since we had spoken of it, but I was sure I had told her. "Why you ain't tell me you was coming to the Dieu house?" she spoke again, this time I could sense a bit if anger in her voice. Mama must have sensed it too, anger and Miss Felix did not go together. "Felix, what is you going on about? We got our baby girl safe and sound. I'm sure it was an innocent mistake. Is she here, baby? Mrs. Dieu, so I can talk to her about you spending the night?"

At that point I wasn't sure what to say. I knew that I would have to confess to Mama about working for Miss Dieu and why. Before I could get a word out Miss Felix spoke, "Mrs. Dieu don't live here no mo'; she went crazy and had to move over to an assisted-care place." Mama and I both looked at her shocked. "How you know that, Felix? Is that true, Thank-You?" Mama spoke to her first, then to me leaving me no choice but to confess, stumbling over my "Y-yes, ma'am. I been coming here to help clean up the place so they could sell the house." I spoke with my head down because I knew Mama was gonna want to know the whole story.

"Mama, when I came to find Mrs. Dieu she was already gone. I was gonna ask her to loan us some money. But instead her daughter was here and offered me a job to help her clean. I was doing it cuz I been knowing Ms. Strongberry wanna take me away from you." I felt relieved to get the truth off of my chest, even though I knew that her feelings would be hurt. I was waiting for Mama to give me a hug and a lecture, but once again before she could speak Miss Felix interjected, "Thank-You, Mrs. Dieu ain't got no daughter." I stared at her for a moment, not quite sure what she was talking about. "Yes, she do, Miss Felix, ma'am. I been working with her for almost two weeks now."

"Well, it looking like somebody trying to steal that poor, crazy old lady stuff, and my baby got caught up in the middle of it," Mama interjected. Her rationale of what was going on made sense, except it ain't feel right. I know what I felt when I was around Josephine, she ain't feel like no crook. "No, Mama, she got a daughter and I met her. She real kind, soft spoken, she got cinnamon skin and freckles that live on her cheekbones up under her eyes. She tell me stories 'bout when she was little. How she used to read right underneath that big oak tree over there." I pointed to the oak tree with the wildflowers living at its base. The more I spoke the paler Miss Felix skin got. She looked like she was ready to pass out. I kept on speaking, hoping to bring some resolve to the situation. "She was here when I fell asleep last night. Maybe she inside still sleeping? It still pretty early." With that Mama, Miss Felix, and me walked into the house. They followed me into the room where Josephine was packing the fine china away the week before. "I'll go look for her," I said turning to walk away.

"Wait," Miss Felix called out, "we shouldn't be in here. This don't feel right." I stopped, not understanding what she was talking about. "Thank-You, Mrs. Dieu had a daughter, but she died. Whoever is here is pretending to be her, and she might be dangerous." I looked at her stunned, that couldn't be true. *Why wouldn't Josephine have mentioned that she had a sister?* I thought to myself. Better yet, how did Miss Felix know all that? "That can't be true, ma'am," I said sure of myself. "Come with me," I boldly stated as I headed toward the staircase, not waiting for them to follow.

As we got to the top of the stairs I couldn't remember the room that I'd found Josephine crying in the night before. There were so many rooms, and it was so dark and dusty that it was impossible to tell. I tried to describe to Mama and Miss Felix what had happened the previous night, hoping that they would believe my story. But Miss Felix who was normally a great listener, wouldn't hear of it. Without realizing she took the lead and led us all down the hallway, she walked directly to the room in which I had fallen asleep in. "Is this the one?" she said, her eyebrows wrinkled in frustration. I nodded in silent response.

As she pushed open the door she fell to her knees and began to cry, leaving Mama and I standing behind her in shock. The room was empty with the exception of the bed and the book which I had fallen asleep reading to Josephine the night before. "Felix," Mama said as she rubbed her back. "What's going on?" Miss Felix looked up at Mama and continued to cry, she wanted to speak but the words were sealed inside of her mouth. "Let's go," Mama said. "No," Miss Felix protested. "There is a reason we here." Standing to her feet with the help of Mama, she made her way inside of Josephine's room as we quietly followed.

"I ain't been here in almost fourteen years," she spoke uneasily. "Josephine Dieu was special to me." She kept on talking as me and Mama listened to her intently, hanging on to her every word. "She was such a sad lil thing when we first met, and as time passed I watched her blossom right before my eyes. She ain't have nobody to love on her, so I gave her all the love I could." As she spoke, her eyes shifted back and forth from sad to happy, reliving every thought as they were brought back to life through her memories. "I would have done anything for Josephine and when she died a big part of me went with her. I was never the same." Her eyes were now staring down at the floor. "Felix why ain't you never tell me 'bout her? Why you kept all this locked up inside yo heart for all these years?" Mama looked sad for her best friend, and a bit betrayed that she had secrets almost as old as their friendship.

"I couldn't tell you, Clara. I couldn't tell nobody cuz, I just couldn't." She stood crying, holding her face in her hands. Mama wasn't sure what to do as we all stood there waiting for clarity. I knew that I had to say something. I knew the truth. When I woke up to the sound of the banging from Mama and Miss Felix everything was a blur, hazy in my mind. But as I listened to Miss Felix speak, the scent of gardenias wafted gently into the room, settling in my nose. After all, these were not only her memories, they were mine as well. I was here with them, listening to the conversations that Ms. Felix Clark would have with my mama about life, love, forgiveness, and faith.

"Mama," my voice coming out powerful. The squeakiness of a child's voice was fading, and I spoke like the young woman that I was becoming. "Mama, Miss Felix couldn't tell you about Josephine, because she was my real-life mama.

43.

Thank-You

They say that a child's imagination is one of the most powerful forces on this planet. As children we are able to tap into the mystery that exists outside of the walls of our minds. We are free from the cage of reasoning and ignorance. We are able to look beyond what is directly in front of us and see the path that lies ahead. As we grow, we begin to lose sight of these things. The mystery becomes overshadowed by the wall that grows bigger with each human experience. Eventually, we forget the magic and wonder that we once found in the belief that anything was possible, and the word impossible becomes the box that we use to shove God into.

I will never be able to prove to anyone that I met my mama. When Miss Felix, Mama, and me left the Dieu house that day we were all exhausted and silent. Miss Felix was unsure of how I discovered the truth, despite me telling her the events that had taken place. I sat in the backseat of her beat-up, old car, the same car that drove us past the field of Southern Magnolia trees to bring me here. To the place where my past met up with my present, lighting the path toward my destiny.

I watched as my breath saturated itself along the dusty glass, as I stared out the barely able to open backseat window. I listened to the wind sneak in through the tiny opening that I was able to create, praying to catch the scent of gardenias in the air again. I know that Josephine was not a dream, a vision brought to life by my hungry imagination. I know that she was real, as real as the two women riding in the front seat of this car.

"Oh Lord," I heard Mama say as we pulled up in front of the house. I turned to see Ms. Strongberry standing on our front porch, face wrinkled with years of stress. Wrinkles that I'm beginning to notice creep their way across my beautiful Miss Felix's face. *Those wrinkles must come with the job*, I think as we park the car. Mama took a deep breath and opened her door, "Let's go, baby girl. It gonna be okay."

I have to be honest, I was afraid. I was grateful that I was able to experience being in the same room with my real-life mama, but I know that she been with me my whole life, and she ain't going nowhere. But Miss Clara, if they take me away, we may never see each other again. The thought causing my knees to shake, as once again she took my little hand in hers. We walked up the pathway with Miss Felix following behind us, not knowing herself what was going to happen.

"Good morning, Ms. Strongberry, ma'am. You here awfully early in the morning. What can we do for you?" Mama's voice ain't shake like mine would have. It's the strength that live up in her bones, that force of wisdom that guides her emotions and thoughts. "Happy to see you got my name right, Ms. Pruitt. I can only stay a minute. I just came by to deliver some interesting news." Ms. Strongberry spoke with a sense of urgency in her voice, and to all of our surprise, there was even a hint of kindness. "There was a package sitting on my desk this morning. It was sent anonymously. I cannot yet disclose the particulars of the case as we have yet to verify all of the facts. But as of right now, Miss Thank-You is the sole beneficiary of the Dieu family trust. I have spoken to the family attorney who has verified that although he did not send the letter, he has known of the child, and if anything were to happen to Mrs. Dieu he were to find her and reveal her entitlement. We are not sure where the letter came from, but it also came with this package for Miss Thank-You."

We listened to her words, standing in disbelief and gratitude. Mama's hands were clasped together as if silently praying. "This discovery affords Miss Thank-You great wealth, and she will need a mother to guide her. She will need you, Ms. Pruitt. The adoption paperwork is being finalized as we speak. Congratulations." It was almost elusive, but I saw the twinkle in her eyes as she was able to deliver happy news causing my arms to react and throw themselves around her waist, catching her off guard. My hug replacing the thank you that simply would not have covered the enormity of my gratitude. Before Ms. Strongberry walked away she placed the small package in my hands. "This is for you."

As she drove off, me, Mama and Miss Felix danced around the front porch as if we was at a grand party. We danced, we cried, and we laughed. "Open it," Miss Felix and Mama said at almost the same time, causing a giggle. I already knew what was on the inside, but I opened it for them. I wanted them to feel it too. I could feel the warmth of a mama's love as I held it tightly, the warmth of all of three of my mamas. I peeled away the first layer of brown paper, the wind brushing softly against my cheek, the smell of gardenias dancing around us all. *"Charlotte's Web,"* I said, showing the book to my mama and Miss Felix, allowing my teeth to feel the wind cuz that's what they love to do.

The End

Made in the USA
Middletown, DE
01 March 2017